TANGENTS & TACHYONS

J. SCOTT COATSWORTH

Published by
Other Worlds Ink
PO Box 19341, Sacramento, CA 95819

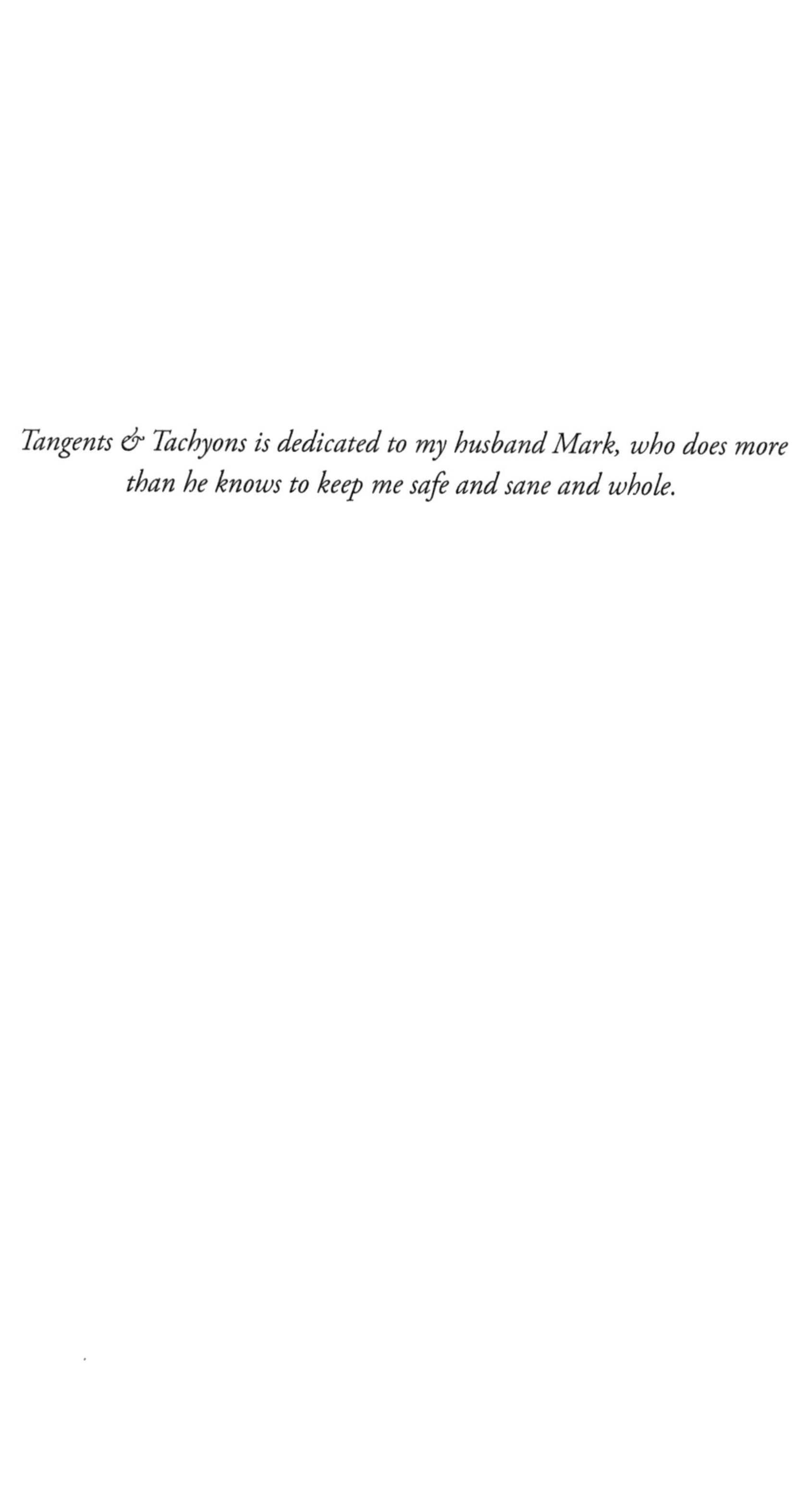

Tangents & Tachyons is dedicated to my husband Mark, who does more than he knows to keep me safe and sane and whole.

CONTENTS

FOREWORD

This is my second short story collection, after 2018's *Spells & Stardust*. Some of the stories in this collection have been previously published in Galaxy's Edge - Across the Transom, Eventide and Lamplighter.

Chinatown and Prolepsis were both self-published as stand-alone short stories.

And Pareidolia is being published for the very first time in this collection.

I've included a little background after each story to provide context about when it was written and what inspired it.

I hope you enjoy these tales!

EVENTIDE

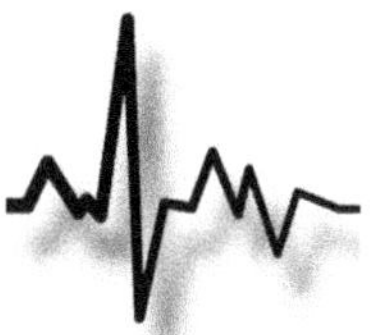

I felt a little sick. Okay, a lot sick—like something had wrenched my stomach out of my gut and pulled it halfway to Mars.

Not far from the truth, as it turned out.

I reached for my stomach. My furry belly was a little thicker than I would have liked—too much processed sugar, Peter said. That and the whole no exercise thing.

What did I eat this time? My memories were a bit fuzzy.

I remembered bright lights and a sharp smell. And a keening whine.

I opened my eyes. The light above dimmed of its own accord.

That's weird. And the smell… kind of antiseptic?

I sat up, and my fingers sank into the soft blue mat beneath me, leaving an impression when I lifted them up which just as quickly disappeared.

I was naked. *What the hell?*

Alarmed, I looked around as my eyesight cleared.

I was alone in a plain white room. White walls curved into a white floor and ceiling, and only the "bed" had any color—a bright blue pad on a raised pedestal. There were no doors or windows.

I pushed myself up and my head spun. My stomach clenched, and I felt sick.

The room swam around me, darkening, changing.

I've been sick. I was certain of that, but the details were vague. I fell back, cushioning my fall with my left hand. "Hello? Peter?"

"Hello, Tanner Black." The reply was warm, cordial. Feminine, maybe? Hard to tell.

"Hello." My head ached. "Where am I? Who is this?" The walls continued to flow.

"I am Sera. You are in an awakening room. Welcome to the Seeker."

"Welcome to *where*?" None of this made any sense. *Where's Peter? He must be looking for me.* I tried to get up again and a searing pain clenched my gut.

"Please lie down, Mr. Black. You have not fully recovered yet, and your room is not ready."

Recovered from what? I wanted to argue, but suddenly resting seemed like an eminently sensible idea. I *was* tired, and my head hurt.

Maybe just a short nap.

I pulled my feet up and lay down, wishing for my comfy feather pillow.

The foam conformed to my body, hugging me. *So comfortable.*

That thought faded as sleep took me, and the light went out.

I WOKE SLOWLY.

I lay still for a while, hoping not to alert whoever or whatever had brought me here to the fact that I was awake.

The last thing I remembered was being in bed, in our little bungalow near the river. With Peter. A strange keening sound rang through my mind, mixed with the smell of hospital disinfectant.

Is this heaven?

I opened one eye, looking at the ceiling.

It was no longer white. Instead, it was coffered, the stained oak paneling that Peter and I had chosen when we'd renovated my den.

I was dressed in khakis and a polo tee.

"Good morning."

I sat bolt-upright, looking around for the source of the voice.

The voice from before. Sera?

She was on the far side of the room, a woman so perfect that I found myself aching at the sight of her in all the wrong places. It was strange. I was pretty much a Kinsey six, a gold-star gay.

Peter and I had joked about the whole "gay men liking hot female celebrities" thing more than once. *"I'd switch teams for Ariana Grande. Voice like an angel."*

That was Peter, ten years younger than me. Always up on the latest thing. Me, I was more of a classic type. *Angelina Jolie, any day.* But this woman? I would have let her have her way with me. *Is that weird?*

Then it struck me. This *was* my den. *How did she get here? How did I? Why can't I remember?*

Sera stood by the window, running her tapered fingers over the books on my bookshelf. She was tall, her skin tawny, her face smooth and unlined, and her eyes were golden and almost too big.

"Good morning....Sera? What are you doing in my house?" Maybe the white room had just been a weird dream.

"Yes. And this is not your house. Not exactly." She set the leather-bound book she'd been leafing through back on the shelf and sat down in the russet-red Tom Ford leather chair in the corner.

I laughed nervously. "Not my house?" What the hell was she talking about?

"It will all make sense soon."

Sure it would.

It was fall outside—the maple leaves outside were red and gold. *Is it November already?* The antiseptic smell was gone, replaced with something like lavender.

"So if this isn't my house…what is this place? Heaven?" Maybe she meant they'd foreclosed on our place, though I didn't remember that. Was she a Realtor? I frowned.

She looked at me strangely for a second, and then smiled. "No. This is neither heaven nor hell. You have some strange concepts."

I didn't know if that *you* meant me, or maybe humankind? Or…? "Where are we, then?" If this wasn't my study, the resemblance was uncanny, right down to the scuff in the bamboo floor where I'd dropped one of my granite bookends.

"We'll get to that. First, let's talk about where you are *from*."

"Dammit, this is hell." Heaven wouldn't keep me waiting like this. *Maybe hell is a waiting room.* Weird how she talked so formally, no contractions.

Sera laughed again. "Really, it is not. Suffice it to say that it's a long time away from your own."

In a galaxy far, far away… That sounded a lot like sci fi. "Is this Milliways? If so, I wanna meet the meat."

Her eyes unfocused again, and then she laughed even harder than before, but her laugh sounded a bit odd. "A surprisingly apt guess."

I hadn't expected *that.* Douglass Adams would be proud. "So am I dead?"

She smiled. It looked like maybe she was trying to reassure me, but it was more like a grimace. "Tell me about where you came from." She seemed eager to press ahead—if she'd had a watch, she would have been glancing at it furiously. "I promise all will be explained."

I sighed. Now this was sounding like therapy. I rubbed my chin, thinking. "My husband and I live in a little yellow house in Sacramento." *Peter, where are you?*

"What's Sacramento like?" She sounded genuinely interested, her fine eyebrow arched.

"It was kind of a cow town. Not as bad now as it was twenty years ago."

Her eyes unfocused, a gesture I was coming to realize meant she was accessing information. "Ah, I understand. Do you like it?" She was taking notes. I could feel it.

I nodded. "More than I thought I would. I came from San Francisco—that's a big city by the ocean. Sacramento is… was?… calmer. Less crazy."

Sera rubbed her chin, looking lost in thought. "And your husband?"

"Peter?" I laughed. "He's a pain in the ass." I couldn't bring myself to talk about him in the past tense.

She started to unfocus.

"It means he's difficult, in an endearing way." Peter was my everything, even if I wanted to kill him at least twice a week.

"I understand."

I looked around again at the den, feeling closed in. Just before this—there'd been a white room like the one I woke up in the first time. Clean, slick, soulless. "I think I was sick."

It was a statement, not a question. There'd been chemo. Weeks of nausea, followed by weeks of recovery.

Sitting in The Chair. The Cancer Club.

Memory washed over me.

. . .

"What you in for?" The skinny woman had a purple bandana wrapped around her head, her freckles vivid on pale cheeks.

I stared at the tube pumping poison into my veins, wishing I were anywhere else. "Prostate. You?"

"Breast." She touched her flat chest, flashing me a mischievous smile. "What do you think of my rack?"

My face flushed. "I don't know…"

"It's all right. Just messing with you. I'm Anna Kirkpatrick."

I nodded, relieved. "I'm Tanner. You have a nice Irish name."

She grinned. "Yes, from my father's side. You?"

"Good British stock. Long time back."

"Welcome to the Cancer Club." She was sweet. We talked about books we'd read, our families, our cancers.

Three weeks later she was gone.

I opened my eyes and looked down at my hands. *Cancer.*

Sera nodded, like a therapist. "Cancer sounds like a terrible thing."

"You don't have it…here?" How did she know? *Where am I? When am I? Is any of this real?*

"No. We did once. Something similar—a cellular malfunction. It was a long time ago."

I looked up, hopeful. "Figured out the secret?" *Maybe they cured me after all.*

Sera looked down at her hands, not meeting my gaze.

"I…I died, didn't I?"

"Yes."

I bit my lip. "So. This is heaven." Sera was an angel. Not that I was particularly religious. And yet, here I was.

"Let me show you something." She stood and touched the

window. It shimmered and changed, the trees and golden afternoon sunlight vanishing.

It was an almost indescribably beautiful vision, hard to render in words.

It was a play of colors, every one of them in the Pantone chart. Or an explosion, sparklers of light playing across the screen. Or maybe a bursting of bubbles.

Or a grand symphony the likes of which Beethoven might have conceived, if he'd worked for Pixar.

It was all of those things, and none of them at all.

I stumbled toward it, reaching my hand out to touch the cool, clear surface. "It's breathtaking." I tried to take it all in.

She nodded. "The screen filters out the escaping radiation. Otherwise you'd be dead."

I already am. I didn't say it. *I should be grateful for whatever this is.*

Mom would have shaken me by the scruff of my neck—*Do you realize how lucky you are?*

Then again, maybe this was all just a dream.

"What is it?" I stared at the strange interplay of colors, the fog and shifting light.

"It's the end of all things." Her lips were set in a grim line.

I stared at her. She looked serious, and also a little broken.

I wasn't good at reading women. I wanted to comfort her, but I held back.

This is *Milliways.* Without the fine dining and self-introductory cows. But the end of the Universe, nevertheless. Or maybe some chemo fever-dream. "Why am I here?"

My stomach rumbled.

Traitor. It didn't matter. *I don't need food. I'm already dead.* Though for some reason, I suddenly had a massive craving for a burger and fries.

Sera touched the window, and autumn returned, though somehow its beauty seemed washed out now. "I'll make you a deal. Let's share a meal. And for every question of mine you answer, I'll answer one from you."

Answers from an angel? Who wouldn't want that? I wished Peter were here to see this. "Deal."

She waved her hand. The alien bed sank into the floor, and in its place, another Tom Ford chair and a small wooden table arose, matched to the stained maple paneling on the walls.

"Fancy." I knelt to examine the table. It was beautiful, hand-crafted. Shaker construction, if I guessed right.

She shrugged. "I suppose. Replication is quite mundane to me. What should we eat?" *Move this along*, her posture said.

There was an aura of sadness around her. I had caught a glimpse of it at the window, but now it was as clear as the autumn leaves.

Outside it was moving from late afternoon into evening.

"What are my choices?"

"Anything you want."

I narrowed my eyes. "You must have quite the kitchen."

She laughed, a little of the sadness lifting. "No, just a good replication system."

"Okay." If this was heaven, it was the strangest version I'd ever heard of. "A McDonalds cheeseburger, fries, and chocolate shake." Everyone knew Mickey Dees had the best fries, even if I didn't eat them anymore. *I am already dead, after all.*

Her gaze went faraway again, and then she touched the bookshelf. After about ten seconds, it split apart, and there was a nook with an orange tray, complete with paper liner and the items I'd asked for. Two of each. "You're joining me?"

She nodded. "When at Rome..."

I laughed, but didn't correct her. Prepositions were a bitch in any language.

I took a bite. *Oh my God.* The cheeseburger was amazing, fake cheese and pickle juice dripping down the side of my mouth. I'd forgotten how good processed food could be.

Sera took a bite and frowned.

"Don't like it?"

"It's...interesting." She pulled off the bun and stared inside. "What's that?"

I squinted. "*That* is a pickle. One of humankind's finest inventions." It took me a second to realize she'd used a contraction.

Sera picked up the pickle and sniffed it. "I'll take your words for it."

I smiled. She was still a little rough on idioms.

I popped one of the fries into my mouth. They were perfect—hot, crispy, salty. And underneath the carton... I stared. "Is that... the Hamburgler?"

Another data check. "Yes, it is."

I laughed. It was patently absurd.

Here I was, vaunted sci fi writer and climate change scientist from the early decades of the twenty-first century, sitting in my den at the end of the Universe, talking pickles with some future human/alien goddess, while a cartoon drawing in a jailhouse jumpsuit grinned at me from a plastic orange tray.

Sera laughed too, and soon we were doubled over squeezing our sides.

"The... the... Hamburglar. And holy shit, Grimace?"

Tears were coming from her eyes. "Why are we laughing?"

"This whole thing...it's just so *weird*."

The laughter trailed off, and we stared at each other in companionable silence.

However different we were, we had just shared a moment. A *human* moment.

I took a sip of the chocolate shake. It was already starting to melt.

"So...ASSUMING I believe what you've told me, what do we do now?"

"Ask me a question." She sat back, her arms resting on the arms of the chair. "Then I'll ask you one."

This was like having a genie. *Do I get more than three questions?* I had to make each one count, just in case. "Can you read my mind?"

Sera shook her head. "Not exactly. I can access a copy of your memories—the one we used to replicate you. It helps me answer some of your questions, and to know what to ask next."

Let's test that. I want to kill you with my bare hands.

I waited to see if she reacted. But she seemed as serene and calm as before. She was either telling the truth, or she was a better actor than me. "Your turn."

"What do your people think about life after death?"

I sat back, staring at her. It wasn't what I'd expected. "That depends. Some of us think there is one. Many of us, actually. There have been many wars fought over different interpretations of that very question."

"And you?"

"That's technically two questions."

She smiled enigmatically and said nothing.

"Well, before today, I would have said no. You get the time you get, and then your atoms are dropped into the cosmic washing machine to be cycled out into something new." *What if I was wrong about that?* Was this place the afterlife, or some kind of elaborate scam?

Sera nodded, giving me nothing.

My turn. "Why am I here?"

"That's a fair question. My kind—you can call us Seekers—we've always sought knowledge across our galaxy. Wherever that search took us. Now that the end is near, think of this as…" That glazed look again. "Ah yes. Our last hurrah."

So I'm a science project. "Okay, but why…"

"*My* turn." Her grin was almost mischievous. "What's Earth like?"

If this whole thing was a chemo dream, it had me fooled.

I closed my eyes. "It *was* beautiful. Lots of wild space, so many animals and plants. When I was a kid, I used to run outside in the monsoon rains barefoot in the street, the pavement rough under my feet, heavy drops falling from the sky. And the creosote smell in the air as the water rushed past." I could still smell that musty odor. I missed those simple pleasures. "Dad took me to the White Mountains once. I snuck out of the tent at dawn to smell the pine needles, and my breath made clouds in the air." I could still see the sunlight filtering like the strings of a harp through the trees. "Can you see it?"

Sera closed her own eyes, and a wistful smile crossed her face. "Yes. It's beautiful."

"It was. We ruined it. Too many people, too much greed."

She stared at me like I was an insect on a pin, her fingers tapping her knee.

Time was growing short. I could feel it. I squirmed. "My turn."

"Go ahead."

"Why me? There are so many smarter people, better representatives of the human race." *Einstein. Mother Teresa. Hell, even Oprah.* My eyes narrowed. "Are you really human?"

Sera laughed. "That's two questions." She rubbed her chin, as if considering how to respond. Just like I had. "You were chosen because you live in a pivotal time for your kind."

"So I'm important?" I scratched my head.

"My turn again." She picked up one of the now-cold fries and nibbled at it. "What's the biggest challenge facing your people?" She sipped her milkshake, waiting for my response.

She looked so *normal*. It made me laugh.

"That's funny?"

"Technically two questions. But I'll allow it." I grinned. "I laughed because you reminded me of a girl I used to date. Before I came out."

Her eyebrow arched, but she didn't ask the question.

"And unquestionably the climate. We've done everything we can to destroy it, and no one seemed to care. I studied these things, and believe me, you'd be scared shitless if you knew half of what I knew." In some ways, it was a relief to be dead—it was no longer my responsibility.

"That's very common. Civilizations often destroy themselves with the very things that lifted them out of the primordial mud." She scratched her head absently.

Just like I did.

"You're really *not* human, are you?"

She set down her shake and her eyes sparkled. Legit sparkled. "No. What gave me away?" Technically it was a question. But it was an answer too.

I was a scientist. I knew the odds. "The end of the universe would be millions, probably billions of years away from my time. The likelihood that humans would still be around to see it… plus you're copying my gestures. Like you're just learning them."

She laughed. "I think I like you humans."

You humans. It was a friendly laugh, but knowing it originated from someone, or something, alien sent a shiver down my spine.

"To answer your question, no, the Seekers aren't human. We never were. We're not really one race at all. Our progenitors evolved on a small world circling a red sun, a billion years ago. After all this time, even the names of our origin race and planet are lost."

I whistled. I had a hard time imaging a million years, let alone a billion.

I suddenly felt very young.

"And to answer your next question…I don't know how old I am. I stopped counting a long time ago. A couple million years? I'm an aggregate—a creature born of a thousand worlds and a thousand cultures that survived their childhoods. Bits of me collected over time, and now I am the sum total of all that came before. All we were able to save. So *age* is a rather meaningless measure, don't you think?"

I stared at her. It was more than I could take in, having a cheeseburger and fries with one of the caretakers of the universe.

She reached out to touch my forehead. "Show me your favorite memory?"

It was like an electric shock.

It was summer, in New York, hot and humid in the way that only the East Coast in July can be, well over ninety degrees and muggy as hell.

I was sitting on a bench in Central Park, in the middle of one of my periodic unsuccessful attempts at getting in shape. It had been a week now and I was still gasping for breath.

Today's attempt had ended badly, with me sitting there panting on the bench, head between my knees, feeling lightheaded and weird.

I was thirty-five and single.

"Want some water?"

I looked up, half-expecting a gym rat, some muscly guy who would drive me back into full-blown body shame.

Instead, he was aggressively *normal.* Light brown hair, brown eyes, nice features, someone you wouldn't think twice about if you saw him crossing Fifth Avenue. He was dressed in athletic shorts, his shirt was tucked into the back of his pants. He had a nice chest, but nothing like you see in the magazines.

Lots of freckles.

"Thanks." I took the water and uncapped the bottle, gulping it down gratefully.

"Hey, don't drink too much. Your body has to play catch-up."

"Not mustard?" I groaned at my own terrible pun. These things just slipped out sometimes.

He must think I was an idiot.

He laughed and held out his hand. "Peter."

I shook it. "Tanner. Tanner Black."

"Oooh. Pornstar name."

"Yeah, well." I gestured at my own lackluster form and shrugged.

He sat down on the wooden bench next to me. "Late New Year's resolution?"

I nodded. "Friend's wedding next month."

"Oh God, I hate those." I handed him back the bottle, and he took a sip. "Gorgeous day." He glanced up at the cloudless sky, a stunning deep blue.

"Damned sweatshop, if you ask me."

Peter laughed again. "Yeah, it is pretty bad." He looked at me, and then looked away again.

"What?"

"Nothing."

"Hey, you wanted to ask me something, or say something. Spit it out."

"Okay." He ducked his head. When he looked back at me, he was biting his lip. "I know it's quick. But… you wanna go out sometime?"

I snorted. *Nobody* wanted to go out with me. "Yeah, right."

"I've been watching you. Not like in the creepy stalkery way. But these last couple days. I was trying to work up the courage to ask you. I know you're way outta my league."

You gotta be kidding me. I'd never had *anyone* tell me I was out of their league.

I looked him over again. He was actually kind of cute, in that quiet, intelligent way I liked. He was funny. And hell, he liked *me*. "Why not?"

He grinned again, and pulled out a sweaty piece of paper from his pocket. "Here's my number. Call me." Then he leaned over and kissed my cheek, got up, and ran off.

I watched him run. He was beautiful.

Maybe the universe had a plan for me after all.

I OPENED MY EYES.

Sera had a lopsided smile on her face.

"What?"

She seemed ever more human. "When was that?"

"Twenty years ago. We've been together ever since."

She nodded.

I felt like I'd just passed a test. "So did we make it?"

"Humanity?"

"Yeah."

She stared at me for a moment, her golden eyes fixed on mine. "Honestly? We don't know yet."

I laughed harshly. "How can you not *know*? This is the end of the universe, right? All the stories have been told."

She bit her lip, a human gesture she seemed to really have taken to. "This isn't *your* universe."

I stared at her. "What?" My head ached.

"You're not really here. Not the original *you*. You and your kind are a thing still to come…" Sera waved her hand, and the window changed again to show the End of All Things. "That's your future, not ours."

I stared at the screen. "I don't understand."

"Our universe is in the final stages of collapse. The Seekers' time is coming to an end. We found a way to reach forward into your universe to continue our mission. Into *your* time, to find places where we might intervene to set young races like yours on a different path before they self-destruct. *If* they are worthy."

"To pay it forward." I was shaking.

Sera's eyes glazed, and when they refocused, she nodded, flashing me a grateful smile.

I had been chosen to represent my entire race. How could I even begin to accept that?

And yet… *humanity must still have a chance.*

I got up and paced around the room, full of nervous energy. "How many?" I demanded. How big was this… ship? This place?

"Races? A hundred thousand or so. Only a small fraction will reach the stars."

"Show me?"

She nodded and took my hand.

My consciousness expanded outside the room.

In the next one over, a creature that looked like a golden beetle

—albeit seven feet tall—chittered with another of its own kind in a room that was best described as *organic*. Beyond that, in a grassy glade, something rustled its purple leaves or feathers in what I had to assume was a query.

As my consciousness expanded, the scene repeated itself over and over, and soon I was swooping up above it all to see the ship.

It was vast, a white amorphous thing, more like a cloud than a hard, physical structure.

It billowed and shifted, all the while being drawn inexorably forward toward its ending.

"Enough." Instantly I was back inside my own body, though I suspected it was no more than alien binary code. I sank back into my seat, overwhelmed by the scale of this effort.

We seemed to have given up on the every-other-question thing, so I plowed ahead. Something else was bothering me. "Couldn't you have just read my mind—or my memory copy—to find all of this out?"

She sat back. "Yes. We could have. We did, in fact. But it was important to see what kind of creature you really are. We find that's easiest when we speak to the being itself. You come to life—you are so much more than just your memories."

That made sense. I noticed she'd switched to plural pronouns. "What about you?"

"What about us?"

"If you could pluck my consciousness from a future universe, surely you could survive the end of this one yourselves."

She looked down at her hands. It was hard to believe that she wasn't human.

"Our time is over. We have accepted that. We've explored all there is to explore." She looked up, and her eyes swirled white, like the ship. "You're at the beginning of your potential. You have so much more to learn and explore. We're jealous."

I laughed. "Some of the physicists say we've discovered almost everything."

"So bold. So confident. You've only just scraped the surface." She frowned. "It's time."

"The End?"

She nodded. "In a few moments, the Seeker will be sucked into the burning heart of possibility, and a few moments later, your universe will be born."

I shuddered. "What will happen to me?" I kicked myself mentally. Her entire race—races?—was dying, and I was worried about myself.

Hell, I was already dead. What did it matter?

"You'll be sent home."

Where I was already dead.

We stood together and watched as the carnival lights engulfed us.

Sera reached out and took my hand as we approached the End. The brightness swelled to unbearability, searing my vision.

She squeezed my hand tightly, fingers warm in mine. Her eyes were wet.

I'd never asked her real name. I opened my mouth…

…AND FOUND myself laying on a bed in a hospital room. Something beeped in a steady rhythm next to me. Sunlight filtered in through pale green blinds.

Peter sat in a chair, bent over, head in his hands.

Was this some kind of after-death, out-of-body experience? *I am dead, right?*

I opened my mouth, but only a croak came out.

Peter looked up, stared at the heart-rate monitor and then at me. His eyes went wide. "Tanner?" He reached me in a second.

I looked at him. "Water."

"Tanner. Holy shit. Doctor Bamra!" Peter ran to the door. "Get the doctor!"

"There's nothing more he can do. Your husband's gone." One of the nurses poked her head into the room to look at me. "You need to—" She squeaked, and almost fell over as I sat up and stared at her. "I'll go get the doctor."

Peter brought me a plastic cup of water.

I felt good. *Really* good. Better than I had in a year. My mind was clear. No more chemo brain. No more weakness or nausea.

Is this a dream?

I closed my eyes, and something blossomed inside me.

The history and thoughts and ideas from a thousand other races who had survived their adolescence flowed through my mind like a flood. The knowledge of a universe.

And Sera's true name. Sera meant *evening* in Italian. Her true name was unpronounceable, but *Eventide* was a more poetic translation.

She'd been the last of her kind.

"How are you alive?" Peter sat on the side of my bed, touching my hand, my chest, my face. "You were *dead*. I saw you die."

The cancer was gone. I knew that, as surely as I knew the charge I'd been given.

There were ways to save us all, to guide the world onto a better path. Even now. "You're never going to believe me."

"Try me."

I kissed him. His face was wet, and he shook as I pulled him into my arms.

"I don't understand."

"I know." I squeezed him tight. "It's going to be okay."

It was our turn to claim the stars.

About Eventide

A FEW OF my recent shorts were inspired by words I ran across that struck me. Sometimes it was because they were completely unfamiliar to me, but in this case, the word "Eventide" is one I've known all my life. But it's not one you hear every day, and there's something romantic about it. I heard it in church one day, and it stuck with me, eventually inspiring this story.

CHINATOWN

Deryn stood next to the ivy-wrapped concrete window ledge, staring out at the twinkling lights of Chinatown in the distance, dominated by the JioJinShan Tower—Chinese for Gold Mountain. A strong wind off the Pacific spun the gyros of the turbines lining the roofs of the shorter buildings, and solar panels sparkled in the late morning light.

In the distance, a skipper drone arose, carrying someone off toward the transport center over in what used to be Berkeley.

Behind him, Gracie scraped bits of burnable refuse she'd been able to glean from the junk vendors in Union Square into the cook pit. "Close the shutters."

Deryn sighed. They'd bonded the year before, and had fallen into a life together, combining his meager earnings as a dreamcaster with her own from the odd jobs she performed in the shells—hollowed out old buildings across the city.

He *really* didn't want to know what those jobs were.

Deryn pulled their makeshift shutters closed. They scraped against the window ledge and slammed together, blocking out the garish light.

Gracie lit the pile of garbage with one of their precious matches. It caught, and soon she had a pot of water simmering over the pit. She slipped in vegetables and a protein cube she'd bought in the square, and the small apartment filled with the delicious smell of cooking.

Somewhere past their thin interior walls, a child cried.

Deryn wiped the table. He pulled out two ceramic bowls from the old plastic cabinet salvaged from a place down on Market Street, setting them in place with care. He sat back on a low cushion and watched Gracie as she cooked. She bit her lip, and unconsciously tucked a lock of her dark curly hair behind her ear.

She was beautiful, her auburn skin marred only slightly by the scar that ran across her cheek like memory-made-flesh—a reminder of rough, lean years in San Jose.

They were saving up bit by bit for her sterilization surgery. Neither one of them wanted to raise a baby in this world, not unless they could both earn a permanent place inside Chinatown.

"They hauled Tess and Jenna before the tribunal last week for a carbon violation."

"That sucks. What did they get them on?" The couple lived on the other side of the floor in the old Macy's building that had become high-demand apartment space for hundreds of Chinatown's low wage workers, former Americans connected to the invaders' enclave.

She sprinkled a little precious salt over the pot. "They were running an old air conditioner on a gas generator."

He whistled. "Hardcore. Where'd they get the gas?"

"Some kind of enzyme they bought from the market. Breaks down plastic, apparently." She pulled the battered pot off the cook pit and ladled soup into each of their bowls.

Deryn poured some of the saved gray water from the morning's dishes over the cook pit. Checking to make sure the fire was out, he opened the shutters again, letting in some fresh air. "I could go for a little air conditioning this summer."

Gracie shuddered. "Not if it means a partial wipe. Their blank eyes… Tess looked broken."

Deryn frowned. He worked for the Chinese. They *were* trying to fix the world, even if their laws were harsh. But mind wiping… there was no world in which extracting bits of someone's brain could be *right*. He sipped his soup, staring at the wall thoughtfully. Burning trash was a minor infraction, but using fossil fuels…

Something buzzed in Deryn's ear. He turned and froze.

A pixie drone had slipped in through the open window and was slowly traversing the room.

He glanced at the cook pit. It was covered. *Thank you, Gracie.* He hadn't even seen her do it.

They sat stock-still while the drone did its impromptu inspection of their tiny living space.

No one knew if the pixies were equipped with cameras or just carbon sniffers, but they were coming around more often lately. The invaders—the Chinese called themselves *rescuers*, but they were invaders nevertheless—had a factory churning them out down in Los Angeles.

The drone fluttered past him, and Deryn could feel the air from the whirring wings on his cheek. It hovered for a moment as if considering what to do with him.

The vein in his temple pulsed.

Seemingly satisfied, it zipped back out the window and was gone.

"That was close." His held breath came out in a huff.

"Too close. That's how they caught Tess and Jenna." Gracie looked calm, but her hands were shaking as she set down the empty soup bowl.

Deryn pulled her close and kissed her cheek. "It'll be okay." He finished his own meal and got up to stare at JioJinShan again. Everyone but the Chinese called it Chinatown.

The invaders had saved the remains of San Francisco, after the superstorms had come and destroyed much of what had survived the Great Collapse. The enclave, with its enormous white tower, offered both food and jobs. Those were low paying, though, and the tensions between the former Americans and the Chinese were palpable.

Deryn felt a lump in his pocket. "Oh, I brought you something!" He pulled out the foil and opened it carefully. They would wash it and save it for re-use. "Li Ming gave it to me." He handed it to Gracie.

She opened it with eager fingers. "Chocolate?" Gracie's face lit up, and she grinned from ear to ear. "Melted, but oh my God!" She pulled over a cushion. "Come sit with me. We'll eat it together."

He moved next to her and shook his head. "Nope, sorry. It's all for you." He would have loved to try it, but the look on her face as she scooped up the melted chocolate and licked her fingers was its own reward.

She finished it, all but the last little bit. "Open your mouth."

"No, I don't need—"

"Open." She glared at him.

He sighed and obeyed.

The sweet, bitter flavor burst in his mouth, bringing back childhood memories. It was *everything* he remembered. Maybe better.

She laughed, a sound he rarely heard anymore. "I have been so craving this lately. Thank you." She put a hand on her stomach, and her eyes met his, the laughter suddenly banished. "I have something to tell you."

Deryn stared at her. Surely she couldn't mean—

"I'm pregnant."

DERYN TRUDGED THROUGH UNION SQUARE, ignoring the hawking cries of the vendors trying to sell him everything from home remedies to fresh vegetables to sex toys.

It was the twentieth of December, and even though the sun had gone down, it was still a sweltering eighty-eight degrees, according to the Chinese-installed time and temperature scroll that ran around the moribund St. Francis Hotel. *Be a good citizen. Save the world! 88 degrees. Be a good citizen...* Deryn spit. Damned propaganda.

I'm pregnant.

They'd agreed that they didn't want to bring a child into this broken world. Was it an accident? Or had she changed her mind? He grunted. *Doesn't matter now.*

The City ended at Sutter Street with a three-story wall that extended east and west around Chinatown, broken only by the Dragon's Gate. As he approached the checkpoint, he held up his *wàn*—under the skin of his wrist—so the sensor could scan it.

Above the gate, something had been painted in precise Chinese characters. His boss Li Ming had told him it meant "All for the Greater Good," a famous line from the Charter. In reality, it could have said almost anything. He wasn't fluent in Chinese, and certainly couldn't afford the memcourse. *Someday.*

The gates swung open before him, and then he was in another world.

Everything in Chinatown was white, clean and new, to better reflect the sunlight and keep cooling costs lower. Even the plants on the rooftops were albino—vegetables and succulents that required very little water, engineered to provide a food source for the colony when crushed and processed.

Deryn stopped in the visitor's office to collect his clothes—plain black pants and slacks marking him as *wàiguó rén* as clearly as his skin. He left his own clothes in a locker.

Dreamcasters worked all hours of the day, depending on where their dreams were most popular. Deryn had managed to grow a decent following in mainland China—dreamwatchers who had a taste for the exotic from across the Pacific.

As he crossed the bustling colony, he could feel eyes upon him. Some were curious, but most were covertly hostile. Wàiguó rén were considered inherently second-class, too stupid to be allowed to be full citizens in the New Society.

After what we did to the planet, who could blame them? Deryn frowned. *Not that they didn't help.* Still, the victors get to write the history.

The Dreamcast Institute building was in the heart of Chinatown, a glass-and-steel dome that looked more like a giant bee hive than a building. His wàn let him inside.

As Deryn made his way through the atrium and its bubbling fountains and lush greenery, he connected to the grid and checked his account balance.

He stopped and frowned. It was fifty yuan less than the day before. He scrolled through the entries in the air above his wrist.

There it was. *Fifty yuan monthly nourishment fee.* Now they were charging him for the food they fed him? He only made forty yuan a shift. *Fucking hell.* He reached the elevator at the back of the atrium and pressed the button for Basement 3, closing his eyes and breathing in deeply to calm himself. Part of him wanted to unload on his boss for this latest injustice.

He held back. By the time he reached her office, he'd managed to calm himself down. He knocked politely on the door, playing the well-trained wàiguó rén.

"Come in."

He opened it and stepped inside. "Ming, I need to talk to you

—" Deryn stopped short. A high ranking official, at least by the medals on his jacket, was sitting across the desk from his boss.

Ming stood and gestured to the newcomer. "Deryn, this is the honorable General Li Cheng. My father."

A general! "Nǐ hǎo." Deryn bowed low, as he'd been taught. "I'm sorry, this can wait." He stumbled backwards out of the office. The last thing he wanted was to get entangled with Chinese brass. Unnerved, he stumbled down the hall and found the dream chamber assigned to him. He slipped inside and palmed the door closed. Taking off his shoes, he closed his eyes again and took a deep breath, mentally preparing himself to lay down and start his 'cast.

The door opened silently. "Deryn?" It was Ming.

He frowned. "It can wait. Really."

"What's wrong? You can tell me." Her brow was creased.

He sighed. "My account. It's fifty yuan lighter today. New fee?"

She nodded. "I'll have it taken off. You're one of our best 'casters. We don't want to… ruffle your feathers—is that right?—before your 'cast."

"Yes." Deryn grinned in spite of himself at her attempt at using wàiguó rén idioms, and sat down on the *chuang*, his dreamcasting couch. "Is there anything else?"

"Just that my father's a big fan. He came from China just to see *you*. Can you meet him after the 'cast?" It wasn't a request.

"Of course. Thank you, Ming." He *was* grateful, and he hated himself for that. Like he was their fucking pet.

He lay back and slipped the feed line into the jack in his neck.

The soft sound of a closing door told him she had gone.

He ran his hand over the stubble on his head, chewed a stick of nico-gum that helped to open up his casting abilities, and slipped into dreamcast mode.

It was well after sunset when Deryn finished his shift. His dreamcast had been a fanciful one with a dark undertone, about the rich inhabitants of a castle in medieval Britain, and the oppressed peasants who scrabbled to get by outside the castle walls.

He hoped he hadn't cut too close to reality with that one.

There *was* a fairy tale ending, a Yaoi thing where the prince finally found his pauper.

The General had made a point of telling Deryn he liked it three times before finally letting him go home, but it had taken another hour working with Ming to get the fee removal paperwork done.

Deryn had put a bit of Daniel in the pauper's character—his chestnut brown eyes and blond hair, his easy grin in the face of adversity. Though Deryn would *never* admit that to another soul. Daniel was five years gone, killed in the short-lived resistance to the Chinese "rescue." A mathematician ill-suited to war—he'd been the last one Deryn had loved before Gracie.

Gracie. It all came crashing back. How were they supposed to support a child in this world? The Chinese claimed they'd conquered climate change, that the Earth's weather would soon stabilize under their rule. But then again, they *said* a lot of things. Even so, Deryn would *always* be second class in this new world order, as would his child.

He climbed the old escalators of the department store. The smell of human waste and the voices of too many people in too small a space assailed him, but he had become used to it. The apartments were ramshackle, but at least each family had their own space.

Some of the other tenants waved to him in passing.

On the seventh floor, Deryn stopped to stare at Tess and Jenna's door.

He wondered what it felt like to be wiped. What was left behind after the punitive process. He shuddered.

He expected Gracie to be asleep, the tiny apartment to be dark. Instead a light shone under the ill-fitting door that he'd recovered it from an old apartment building in SOMA. It had never fit really well—he was no carpenter. "I'm home—"

"We have company." Gracie met him at the door and gestured to the man she was talking to.

The blood drained from his face. It was General Li. "Nǐ hǎo." He bowed.

The man nodded but didn't get up. "Nǐ hǎo. Come, sit. We have much to discuss."

"I CAN'T DO IT." Deryn stared at the General. The man was insane. He had to be, to have come up with such a mad plan. *And to expect me to help him.*

The general nodded. "You could run—I wouldn't come after you. But where would you go?" He picked up the stick by the covered cook pit, looking at the darkened tip. "Your *America* is gone. Nothing but hunger and famine and misery left. And it would be a shame to lose such a talented dreamcaster."

Gracie looked at him, her hand slipping to her belly. "I heard things were better up in Spokane—"

The General grunted. "I'll save you the trouble. Spokane's a desert. Bad burn a couple years back wiped it out. I'll say it again. Your America is *gone*." He threw the stick out the open window.

Deryn watched it disappear into darkness. "Is it really so bad? Maybe they'll just let things continue on as they are…"

The General shook his head. "I've seen the plan." He was being cagey but seemed genuinely worried.

"They'll kill me if I do it."

The General nodded. "Maybe."

Gracie shook her head. "We'll take our chances on our own. Deryn, you don't have to do this."

"You have someone else to think about now, don't you?" The General's gaze slipped down to Gracie's stomach.

"How did you—"

"Where do you think she got tested?"

His eyes met Gracie's, and she blushed. "I had to be sure."

"Those results are supposed to be confidential."

The General laughed. "Wàiguó rén getting free health care can't expect privacy too."

Deryn snorted. "If… and I am not agreeing… if I do this, when would it happen?"

"Tomorrow on your regular shift. I can't stay here too long, or I'll arouse too much suspicion."

"Why can't *you* do it?"

The General frowned. "If I could, I would. It has to be a dreamcaster. You're one of the most popular dreamcasters we have. The Chairman loves your 'casts."

"He does?"

The General nodded. "And last week, you reached two billion souls with your San Francisco Summer of Sixty-Nine cast."

Deryn blinked. *Two billion people.* He couldn't comprehend such a number. All of them watching his art.

"You've stoked quite a bit of sympathy in China, you know."

Deryn gulped. When he dreamed, it was just him in the chamber. He had no idea he'd reached so many, or so deeply. "And you're sure about this plan? About all of it?"

The General nodded. "I give you my word."

Deryn sat back against the makeshift wall of the flat. "If they take me away—"

"Deryn!" Gracie's eyes were fire.

He pushed ahead. "If it happens, you *have* to take care of Gracie."

"Done." The General waved his hand over the floor between them, and a glowing contract appeared, all in Chinese.

"What does it say?" Deryn peered at the squiggly characters.

"What we agreed upon. Would you believe me if I told you?" The General raised an eyebrow.

Deryn laughed harshly. "Not really."

The General nodded and leaned forward. His thumbprint left behind his own personal chop—his signature under Chinese law. "Your turn."

Deryn reached out for Gracie.

She took his hand.

"What do you think?" His head was spinning. This was all happening so fast.

"I don't—*you* have to choose. There's no way to know."

Deryn nodded. He took a deep breath, and before he could change his mind, reached out and affixed his thumbprint to the contract.

Wàiguó rén were not allowed to have a chop.

In for a penny, in for a dollar. Whatever a penny was. "Well, General Li—"

"If we're working together, you should call me Cheng."

"Cheng." It sounded wrong. "Did you really come here because you liked my dreams?"

Cheng studied him for a long moment. "Not… exactly. You *are* very talented. I chose you for that reason, among others. And because of the Chairman. And because you seemed to have… reasons to co-operate." Cheng handed Deryn something.

Deryn held it up to the light of the glow sphere. It looked like the end of the cable that plugged into his jack. "What is this?"

"It's a splice. You'll need to smuggle that in with you. Use it with your jack." He handed over something else. "Here's a skin patch too, to cover it."

Deryn stared at the tan thing—it looked like an old bandage. He held up the splice. "What does this do?"

"You'll get your instructions when you plug in." Cheng stood and assayed a short bow. "I'll leave you now." He bowed, lower this time. *Respect.*

Comforting. Deryn shook his head. "I hope this doesn't get me killed."

"You are doing me and your people a great service. One day you'll realized that. If you survive."

DERYN WAS SWEATING PROFUSELY.

Security at the Dragon Gate was beefed up significantly—normally he just auto-scanned his wàn and was granted access. But today everyone entering Chinatown was being subjected to a full body scan by human guards, creating a significant line down Grant Avenue that wound through piles of rubble from an old collapsed brownstone shell.

A few blocks East, the Seawall held back the San Francisco Bay, keeping it from flooding at high tide.

Deryn rubbed the skin patch on his thigh worriedly. It was supposed to make anything underneath it undetectable to scanners. That was great in theory, but not so reassuring when you were staring into the hard face of one of the Imperial Guard.

His turn came at last. "Nǐ hǎo."

The guard ignored his attempt at pleasantries. "Arms up."

Deryn did as he was told, wondering what the penalty for smuggling contraband *into* Chinatown was. Smuggling it out got you a wipe and reset. Surely bringing something *in* wasn't as bad? Unless it was a weapon. *It's not a weapon, is it?*

Her wand paused by his crotch.

Deryn shivered. *Too close.*

"Please empty pockets."

Deryn did as he was told, taking out his ID card and the stick of nico-gum he used to help awaken his senses before a 'cast.

The guard took the gum, holding it up. "This is forbidden." She started to throw it away.

"Wait! I have a special permission from Li Ming at the Dreamcast Institute. It's on file."

She stared at him, then nodded. "One moment." She tapped her temple, and her eyes went dull for a moment. When they refocused, she handed him back the gum. "Please carry permit, next time."

"I will. Xiè xiè."

This time there was a glimmer of something warmer in her eyes. "You welcome." She waved him through. Her English was pretty good, but he pegged her as new in town.

He changed into his black clothes and hurried along the crowded but strangely subdued streets. While never popular in Chinatown, he felt something different today in the way people looked at him. Or didn't. The majority simply turned away, but some stared at him as he walked by, and one woman shook her head and sighed before he passed out of sight.

A little girl bumped into him and looked up. Her mother, holding her hand, whispered "*Zhuī mèng zhě.*"

." He knew that one. *Dreamcaster.*

She touched his cheek. "I am sorry," she said in perfect English. Then she was gone with the crowd.

Sorry? Sorry for what? *What's happening?*

He reached the Institute and found Li Ming in her office. "Ming, what's going on?"

She looked up at him, her face seeming more pale than usual. "What do you mean?"

"The security, the glances. People look spooked. Or worried… or maybe sad. What's up?"

"Nothing for you to be concerned about." She looked back at her desk, swiping a stack of virtual papers off into the ether.

She was a terrible liar.

"Ming…"

She stood, her hand going to her hair to check that it was still in place, every move economical, necessary. When she looked back up at him, her eyes were wet, but her voice was firm. "Nothing. Just do what you've been told. Now leave me be. I have a lot of work to do today."

He started to object, but something stopped him. The look in her eyes. "Of course, Li Ming." He bowed and backed out of the office.

She couldn't talk about it. She was being watched. *Just do what you've been told.* She *knew.*

Deryn trusted her. Implicitly. She'd always backed him up and was as tough as nails. If something had *her* spooked…

He shook his head. He was committed. All he could do now was move forward.

Deryn reached his assigned cubicle and closed the door behind him. He slipped off his shoes and pulled down his pants halfway, feeling for the patch on his thigh. At his touch, it fell away from his skin, falling to the ground and sizzling into nothing.

He looked around the small white room. Certainly there were cameras in here, watching his every move.

He had to trust Ming.

He pulled the splice off his leg, taking a few hairs with it.

Grimacing, he found his feed line and attached the splice to the end.

Then he chewed on the stick of gum and lay back on the couch, staring at the white ceiling. After a moment's hesitation, he plugged the line into the jack on his neck.

His world exploded in color. Thoughts that weren't his own wormed their way into his mind. He fought back, striving to close off his brain, pushing them back into the splice. Then he saw them for what they were. Not an intrusion. *Knowledge. Instruction.* Like a memcourse.

Deryn let down his defenses and they flowed into him, constructing a whole framework inside his head. It was like the learning maps Ming had allowed him to access, but more focused, more technical. His mind connected them with his own knowledge, and soon he understood what they wanted.

To steal the Chairman's dreams. Or more specifically, one of his memories.

Deryn sat up, yanking the cable out of its socket, and the whole construction collapsed in his head like one of the buildings along Market Street, leaving in its place a pile of rubble.

He gasped for breath, closing his eyes and trying to calm himself.

They wanted him to steal something from the mind of the most powerful man on Earth. An act that would surely have consequences far beyond a wipe and re-set.

He took a deep breath, then another and another, struggling to calm himself. *How the hell did I get into this mess?* The General had promised to take care of Gracie if he went through with it. To make sure she was safe, that she and their child could have a good life. Deryn sighed, his breath coming out in a rush.

He *knew* then that he would do it.

He hadn't planned to become a father. But now there was a

piece of him coming into the world that needed protection. If he ran, he'd condemn Gracie and their child to a life of misery and starvation. Or worse.

Deryn opened his eyes. *I can do this.*

He laid back on the foam *chuang* and plugged back in, and the construct re-formed in his mind's eye.

The Chairman was a fan of his casts. Cheng had told him as much. Through the splice, Deryn would be able to reach him.

He would spin a cover dream, something pleasing that would keep his prey lulled to sleep. Then he would sneak into the Chairman's mind like a thief in the darkest night and take what the General wanted.

Deryn cast about for suitable dream material. Something historical. Chinese. Something valiant with beautiful women… *Got it.* Chen Jian, daughter of the Empress of a Thousand Stars, and her lover Lin Ju-Long. The lesbian couple were a fan favorite, a big crowd pleaser.

He closed his eyes and spun the dream:

Chen Jian walked through the gardens of the royal palace in Beian…

As his dream unspooled, he swam up-current, exploring parts of the grid he'd previously only surmised must exist.

His splice must have some serious blackware shit inside—it gave him unfettered access to the grid and led him along the conduit like a fish swimming upriver.

The data path was like a multi-forked stream, splitting and recombining, bits of data aggregating to form smooth flows and then breaking apart again in a spray of sparks—a beautiful three-dimensional river, surrounded by dark, hulking towers of processing power. It flung him forward, plunging into one of those towers and flinging him up into the heavens.

Some part of him remained behind, casting the dream, but this part thrilled to the wild ride through the network.

He supposed his consciousness must be flying through space by now, across the Chinese microsatellite network that supported the grid and connected the far-flung New Society back to mainland China. He fancied himself an astronaut, a space explorer, riding high above Earth and all of its troubles.

Then he was hurtling back down toward… something.

To his virtual senses, it was a vast, brightly lit amusement park of lights, something like Disneyland must once have been—one of the places his mother had told him about as a child. *The happiest place on Earth.*

The place expanded below him, growing from speck to island, then becoming as vast as a continent. Suddenly he knew what he was looking at—the heart of the grid, the homeland network that ran China's virtual world.

He slipped into it like a hot knife into grease, and then shot off at a ninety-degree angle from his previous path.

All around him, great rivers of data moved and surged and combined, but here they were rainbow colored, forming tight coils and lazy bends, as beautiful a geometry of movement as he had ever seen.

It would have made Daniel's little mathematician's heart sing.

Deryn slowed, closing in on his target. The river he was following constricted, flowing through a linked series of gateways. *Security checks.* A man of the Chairman's importance wouldn't leave his own mind undefended.

The flow ground to a halt.

Deryn cast his perception around, nervous.

Just ahead, the river glowed an angry red inside one of the

gateways, and with a flash a batch of data vaporized, burning away like smoke that quickly vanished.

Then his forward motion began again.

This is too dangerous. Deryn tried to backpedal, to go back the way he had come. He didn't know the rules here. They said if you died in your dreams, you died in real life too. He suspected that was a bunch of bullshit, but what happened if the system vaporized this part of him?

Still the flow carried him inexorably forward.

He wanted to close his eyes, but he had none, only an awareness embedded in the flow.

He passed through the last gateway, waiting to die, and somehow emerged unscathed. If he'd had lungs, he would have breathed a huge sigh of relief.

Up ahead, the stream flowed into a black hole. As he was carried into it, his world broke apart, and he was Deryn no more.

Slowly Deryn's consciousness reassembled himself, and he became aware of his surroundings again. He was in a fairyland. A dark fairyland.

His heroines Chen Jian and Lin Ju-Long swept past him, off on a quest to find the sacred oracle. He grinned at that. It was a bit cheesy, but his fans ate that shit up.

As he got his bearings, he became aware of other, grimmer things. Shadows that slunk around him in the darkness. Foul smells like rotting corpses. Creaking memories that emanated blackness like light.

He knew what he was after. Or at least *when*. The sooner he found it, the sooner he'd be out of there. He accessed the Chairman's personal calendar, looking for the memory code that would let him find that moment. All the while, strange things spun around him in the shadows, sending a shiver up his virtual spine.

A CHILD on a bicycle making his way along the crowded streets of a Chinese metropolis, the skies filled with smog so thick he could have cut it into bricks.

Colorful carp in a vast ornamental pond surrounded by bamboo, leaping across one another in a feeding frenzy that made the water boil.

The dark slash of a knife and a spray of blood that filled his virtual senses with a metallic sticky tang.

AND THEN HE WAS *THERE*, in the memory he sought. He understood the language as if it was his own—because for the moment it was.

~

"ARE WE READY?"

His second in command—a man he simply called his first general—nodded and submitted the plan. It had been written by hand, committed only to paper. It was too dangerous to allow it to be hacked on the grid.

The Chairman leafed through it. It contained projections—costs, expected casualties, time frame for completion. He took a deep breath and sighed, deeply saddened by the necessity of the solution proposed. His own people were a model of efficiency, having taken to the strictures the party enforced. A liberal society flourishing under absolutely necessary harsh daily life. Carbon levels were leveling off, even falling in Chinese-controlled territories.

But it wasn't *enough*.

Reduced to primitive living, the wàiguó rén created far more carbon with their burning of anything they could get their hands on than they were worth. For the sake of the rest of humanity—for the sake of the Earth—they had to go. The alternative was death for the whole planet.

He set down the folder, looking at his generals expectantly.

"Let it begin."

THE MEMORY ENDED. Deryn was shaken to the core.

"Who are you?"

He was his virtual self again. He looked up into the Chairman's eyes. The man was much less imposing in his night clothes here inside his own mind than in the tricasts Deryn had seen, but his face was hard as stone.

"Just a pauper in the court of Jian Chen." He spun around and did a little dance, his guts churning with his newfound knowledge. *They're planning genocide.*

The man smiled and clapped his hands. "Sing a little song for me. The love song."

Deryn racked his brain. *The love song?*

Then he knew. He called it Jian's song, a melancholy spell of love and heartache. He spun it out, hoping he remembered it all.

SHE SITS upon her mother's throne
and stares at the cherry-blossom sky…

THE CHAIRMAN SWAYED to the music like a little boy, and slowly faded from sight. *Falling back asleep, thank God.*

As soon as the man's spectre was gone, Deryn fled. He felt dirty. Soiled. The secret knowledge he carried would have consequences for millions. And for two people in particular—Gracie and his child.

He held on tightly to the documents he'd stolen. All that mattered now was getting it home—

Heat seared him, red light flaring around him like he was in a house on fire, his mind aflame as one of the security gateways sought to burn him to ash.

Caught. The pain sent him spinning down into nothingness.

DERYN BLINKED. The world around him was blurry, white.

Someone was peering down at him. His mind struggled to put a name to that round, friendly face. *Ming.*

"Did you get it?"

He shook his head. "They caught me. Oh God. Gracie! Is she safe?"

"She's protected, for now. But if you didn't get it, we're all in grave danger." Her father Cheng's voice sounded tired, defeated.

"I'm sorry." Deryn pulled out the cable and the splice and sat up, rubbing his temples. He could still see it. That horrid document…

He could still *see* it. "Wait. Give me a sec."

"What?" Ming and her father said in unison.

He pulled the splice off the end of the cable and plugged it in. "I think—just give me a sec." He brushed Ming's hand away and closed his eyes.

The splice had a buffer cache, he was sure of it. Probably to keep the copy of "him" refreshed as he moved through the network.

He parsed it, and grinned. The memory was *there*, in the cache. "I… I think I have it."

He opened his eyes to find Cheng staring at him. It was still strange to think of him in such familiar terms.

"Did you… understand what it said?"

Deryn nodded, the blood draining from his face. "Yes. I did. Genocide"

"Yes." Cheng glanced at his daughter. "You have to give it to me."

"I can't. He'll kill me. And Gracie. And you too." *And our child.*

"Not if we use it as leverage." Ming sat beside him, taking his hand in hers. "What he wanted to do… it goes against the Charter. You know about the Charter."

He nodded. The original document of the New Society. The one that had given the Chairman almost unlimited power to do what had to be done to save China and the world.

"The Chairman… what he wants to do, it's not permitted. He has abused the Charter in many ways, large and small. But genocide…" She shuddered. "This is not permitted. He wanted to do it anyway and apologize later. Or just bluster through. But with this evidence…"

"How will you prove it's real?"

Cheng pointed to the splice. "With that. If it has the document, it has his own personal mental imprint too. We can use that against him. May I…?"

Deryn pulled away. "Why was everyone looking at me so strangely today when I came here?"

Cheng and Ming exchanged glances.

Ming responded, her face pulled tight. "The plan… it began this week. In Los Angeles."

Holy fuck. "What happened?"

Cheng looked like he was on the verge of tears. "They called it an uprising. After they isolated the wàiguó rén, they gassed the rest in the warrens around the new city."

Like rats. He touched the splice. "So they think I'm a rebel? That's why they stared at me?"

Ming shook her head. "No. They think… the rumors are flying about an extermination. But there's no proof. We think the Chairman will wait for them to die down and then—"

"I get it." Deryn felt sick. His people wouldn't stand a chance. The world was big, bigger than he'd been able to imagine from his tiny flat in the old department store building. And more dangerous.

Still, now he had leverage.

He took the splice out of its socket and held it in his hands. He could drop it to the ground and crush it in an instant. He looked up at Cheng. From the way the man watched the splice in his hand, Deryn could see that he knew it too. "What happens to the Chairman?"

That shared look again.

Ming squeezed Deryn's free hand. "We push him out. We have… friends in high places. With that report, we can force the formation of a new government. We can—"

"Who will be the new Chairman?"

She started and turned to look at her father.

"I will."

Deryn blanched again.

Here, sitting in front of him, was the man who might soon be the effective leader of the world. Suddenly *Cheng* seemed a wildly inadequate form of address.

"I know this is confusing for you," Cheng said, his voice steady. "But you have to decide. Now. Most likely they are already onto us. Your incursion won't have gone entirely unnoticed, and I have been watched for some time." Cheng's voice was calm but pulled tight as a sitar string.

Deryn looked into Ming's eyes. He could trust her. And by extension, her father. *If I'm wrong…*

It didn't matter. He would never have more power than he did at that moment.

Besides, they could have taken it from him, stunned him and pried it out of his hand, maybe before he had time to break or damage it. If they'd wanted to. The fact that they hadn't tried… He nodded. "I'll give it to you."

A visible wave of relief passed over Cheng's features.

Deryn savored his momentary importance. "I have some conditions."

THE NEXT FEW hours passed in a blur. Once Deryn relinquished the splice to Cheng, trading it for a signed and registered contract agreeing to his demands, he was whisked off through the halls and up to the roof, where a waiting skipper drone lifted him and Ming away from JioJinShan.

It was close to midnight.

She waved at her father below as the drone climbed into the sky and veered off across the colony and old city toward the San Francisco Bay.

He'd never ridden in a skipper before. It was magical to soar above the ground this way, like a bird, seeing the Seawall pass beneath them as they soared out over the bay below.

"Thank you for helping us." Ming stared out the window at the water below, her face a solemn mask.

"I should be thanking *you*." Away from the office, she looked less like his supervisor and more like just another human being.

"He is risking everything to change things."

"So are you. You're a hero."

She turned to stare at him, and then nodded. "I guess that's true." She reached out and squeezed his hand. "I don't feel like one."

Join the club. They were silent the rest of the trip.

The craft carried them to a small rocky island in the middle of the bay. His mother had told him about this place once, a prison that held some of society's most hardened criminals.

Several men in crisp white suits helped him climb out.

Ming hung behind. "I'll come back for you when it's over." Her hand shook on the door handle.

"Where are you going?"

"Back to help him."

He scratched his head. "I thought he wanted you safe. *Here*."

She nodded. "It's not his choice to make." The door slid closed, and the drone lifted off again, bound for Chinatown.

Deryn wondered if it was the last time he'd ever see her.

One of the men led him into the old prison. "I'm Steve. I'm your bellhop. I'm here if you need anything."

Steve? Bellhop?

The man must have noticed his confusion. "My parents were Chinese-American. It's been… quite an adjustment from American to Chinese overlord." He grinned.

Inside, the prison had been refurbished. A wide bamboo reception desk ran along one side of the ornate lobby. The other guests stared at him as he passed, but no one said a word.

Steve took him up a flight of stairs, and at the door to one of the old cells, he held up his wàn. The door slid open smoothly.

"Prison, huh?" Deryn flashed him a sardonic grin.

"Not at all, sir. You've been given full hotel access."

Deryn blushed. "Thanks." He stepped inside the luxurious suite, nothing at all like he had expected. Plush black carpets and beautiful white hand-crafted bamboo furniture—sustainable like everything the Chinese did—gave the room a rich feel. But he only had eyes for Gracie.

"What happened?" She flung herself at him, pulling him close. "They wouldn't tell me anything. I was so worried. Are you okay?"

"Need anything else?" Steve was grinning at the two of them.

"No, we're good."

"Nothing will happen to you while you're our guests." Steve closed the door behind him.

Deryn looked around. It was the most luxurious room he'd ever seen—large, clean, full of real wood furniture. "Is there… a shower?"

"Yes. It's wonderful." Gracie grinned. "It's wonderful."

It was Deryn's turn to grin.

"Now tell me what happened!" Gracie pulled him to the couch, and they sat facing each other, her hands in his.

"Okay, the short version. The long one can wait until I get a nice, hot shower."

DERYN WAS asleep on the almost-too-comfortable bed with Gracie in his arms when an insistent ping tone woke him. He sat up, blinking in the bright sunlight. The clock said 11 AM.

"What's that?" Gracie sat up, rubbing her eyes.

"Someone's here. Don't move until I call for you." Despite Steve's assurances, he knew nothing would save them if Cheng's gambit failed.

He crept up to the heavy door. "Who is it?"

"Ming."

Deryn hesitated. He couldn't be sure it was really her. Then again, if it wasn't, they were dead already.

He ran his wàn over the scanner. The door opened.

"Who is it?" Gracie stood at the bedroom door, ignoring his instructions.

"My boss, Li Ming." He ushered her into the room. "Ming, this is Gracie."

Ming bowed to Gracie from the doorway.

"So?" Was it time to run?

Ming grinned. "It's over. We won."

DERYN STOOD on the terrace of the Macy's Building. Behind him, crews were busy converting the old shell into actual livable apartments, shoring up its walls in the process. It was the first of many planned projects to bring civilization to the wàiguó rén, personally approved by Chairman Li upon his ascension to the Chair.

Soon there would be a path to citizenship for Deryn's people in the New Society.

He and Gracie had moved into their own apartment the week before, and he was supervising the project.

It was cheaper and better to reuse the shells than to use the resources and energy to build something brand new, and Gracie was helping them source raw materials to make recycled furnishings.

"How's the park coming?" Gracie slipped her arm around his waist. She was showing.

He looked down at Union Square below. "The first of the modified trees are being planted tomorrow." The gene-grafted trees would suck twice the carbon out of the atmosphere as their natural counterparts.

Deryn set a hand on her stomach.

Gracie's face lit up. "Feel that?"

He laughed. "She kicked me."

"She likes you."

Deryn sighed contentedly. The new San Francisco and JioJinShan would grow together, and his people would get new homes *and* learn how to protect their world. For the first time in years, Deryn had hope. "Daniel would have loved this." He'd always excelled in creating order from chaos.

She squeezed him tight.

He glanced at her protruding belly. "We have a whole new world to build for her."

She nodded. "I always *knew* we could do it."

He turned to stare at her. "You always said you didn't want kids."

"I said I didn't want to bring kids into *that* world." She gestured at the square. "This one is different."

He nodded and kissed her forehead. "It will be."

About Chinatown

San Francisco's Chinatown is one of the older parts of town. Visiting it is a bit like stepping back in time, and away from the high tech culture of The City.

The speculative fiction writer posited a future world where Chinatown was the most technologically advanced place in San Francisco, and how that might have happened. A world where China is the dominant world power, and drones search for carbon violations and punish them accordingly.

But as with most of my stories, there has to be hope, too, right? And so "Chinatown" was born.

THE FROG PRINCE

"Holy crap."

Jillian Tinsnip's spell had gone horribly awry.

He was a bit of a crap magician to begin with. He was always leaving his wand back at the apprentice dorm when it was time for his Witchery & Wizardry course, and just last week he'd accidentally turned the rest of his class into frogs when he was trying a spell to conjure himself up a fair prince from a swamp toad.

It had taken Mistress Vroben a good three hours to disenchant everyone back to their normal selves, and Jory Klemp still walked with a bit of a hop.

But this... this was far worse.

All the hillsides before him had taken on rainbow hues.

He pushed his thick glasses back up onto the bridge of his nose and looked at the spellbook he'd stolen from the Mages wing of the library. He'd been looking for a spell to make himself more handsome. This one had said it would bring out his "inner beauty," whatever the heck that meant.

He sounded it out again under his breath.

"*Or su gah fo pash.*" Damn. He'd said "*goh*" instead of "*gah,*" he was sure of it.

"Hey Jillian."

Jillian stiffened. "Um, hey Jory." He had a bit of a secret crush on the captain of the Sticky Wicket team

Jory hopped up beside him. "Wow. You did this?"

Jillian blushed. "Um, yeah, about that—"

Jory whistled. "It's beautiful."

Jillian exhaled. He hadn't expected that."You… you think?"

Jory nodded. "The hills are much better this way." He grinned. "You must be really strong to do something like this."

"Um, sure?" Jillian pushed a stray lock of hair behind his ear.

"I know you probably get asked this all the time..." Jory blushed.

Nobody asked him anything. Hardly ever. "What?"

"Would you go out with me sometime?"

Jillian's mouth fell open, but he slammed it shut before Jory noticed. He *hoped.* "Um, sure," he said as nonchalantly as he could manage. He nudged his glasses back up again.

Jory grinned, and it lit up his whole face. He took Jillian's hand, and they started back toward school together. Jory hopped with joy.

Jillian glanced back at the rainbow-colored hills.

Well, at least one of my spells worked. I got my prince.

About The Frog Prince

In 2017, Boy Meets Boy asked me to write a flash fic piece and gave me a few photos to choose from as inspiration. I chose a picture of a man staring out at a bunch of rainbow-colored hills, decided it was about a

clummsy wizard-in-training, and the rest just wrote itself. You can see the original image here:

https://www.jscottcoatsworth.com/flash-fiction-the-frog-prince/

ACROSS THE TRANSOM

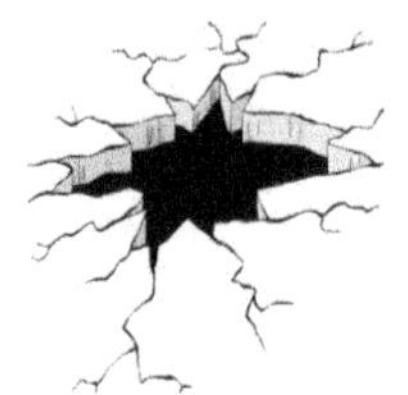

You wake screaming, but no sound comes out of your mouth. *Don't be afraid. I won't hurt you.*

It's a regrettable part of the transfer. I wish it were different, but I have only a few seconds to cross the transom, and no time to make it easy.

I enter you.

Our eyes flicker open.

I can feel the frightened fluttering of your heart. *Our* heart.

We are one now. Your body, my soul. You are my puppet. I am truly sorry it had to be you. I don't get to choose.

We reach down between our legs, and our body quickens at our touch. It's soft there. Warm. Our body is covered with pliant pink skin. Four limbs. A head covered with hair.

Not scaled, like the last time.

Time. Time is short.

I can't get distracted by your needs and fears. This has to be it—I have to stop *Him* this time. I owe Aiaia that much.

We get up, slipping out of bed, leaving your mate alone under the coverings.

His fleshy, hair-covered arm is splayed across your pillow. Oblivious of what's happening to you. To us.

You wail in protest, but you have no control, no voice to scream with.

I can feel *Him* coming. The disruptor, destroyer of worlds.

He's here now too. On *Earth.*

I roll the name across our tongue. It's a strange word, but beautiful enough. Exotic.

We don't have much time. I remind myself. There can be no distractions. Transfer is always disorienting, for the host and for me.

We must stay focused, you and I.

We are crying now, a strange sensation as warm water runs down our cheek. I force us to stop, and we wipe our cheeks dry.

This will go easier if you stop fighting and surrender to me. I won't hurt you.

I feel you retreat inside of us.

Our shoulder itches. We reach up to scratch it absently with our strange configuration of five fingers.

Fumbling quickly through your closet, we find clothing. *Jeans. T-shirt.* You supply the words, your fear slumping to a dull, thrumming ache.

"What are you doing?" Your mate is awake. *Kevin.* Another male of your species. *Humans.*

I gather only the information I need from your mind. "Go back to sleep. I'm going for a walk." The words, though alien to me, seem to make perfect sense to him.

Kevin nods. "Be careful." He lays back down, and soon a heavy, rhythmic sound emanates from him.

Snoring.

This is something you do sometimes—you are restless, like me.

I can see it in our head. Hundreds of walks on different nights, all down the same street. *Streets. Not airways.*

The moon high above, or the halo of light panning the street and *Mrs. Neely's* well-trimmed *photinia* hedge, its new red springtime leaves glowing golden in the light of the *streetlamp*.

So many new words. I shake our head. No more distractions. Last time, he got there mere seconds before I did, and she was lost because of it. *Let's go*. We nod. Together, we slip out of the room and out of the residence.

We stop to stare at the stars. *You have a beautiful world.* I can feel your thrill of pleasure. Lovely growing plants fill your neighborhood—trees, bushes, grass and flowers. The air is cool and fresh on our face.

It's nothing like my own world. *Burnt* and *blasted* are two of the kinder adjectives I could use. The heat suited me, though, finding relief in the higher climes. Aeries reaching halfway to the stars.

~

YOUR *CAR* IS in the driveway. How quaint to have your own mode of transportation. You must live in a time of great riches.

We slip behind the wheel, and you start the car.

I miss my wings.

My unerring sense of direction is quickly merging with your own knowledge of this world. I'm lucky this transfer—your mind has a knack for maps and streets and how things fit together.

Maybe this time things *will* be different.

When I transfer across the transom, I never know who I will enter, what skills they will have. Or how well they will take to the merger.

Some fight me until it's too late.

I feel you shiver inside of us at the thought.

Don't be frightened.

If we survive this, you will be as you were before, and I'll be gone. Or after *Him* again on the next world.

It's dark out, and the streets are empty this early in the morning. We roar down Gage Court to Village Green Drive, and then out the gates, peeling around the corner onto the *parkway*.

We're headed into the city.

Sacramento.

That feels right.

With any luck, *He* will find a poor host this time, one who will hinder Him more than help him. From your mind, I can see that your world is full of these. Humans who don't know how to think for themselves.

No, I don't know his name. Only the burning coals of his eyes, the anger and hatred for life and order and progress that fuels *Him*. He is entropy, darkness, a primal scream against the organized structure of life and the universe.

But sometimes *He* is his own worst enemy. I hope for our sake that this is one of those times.

You feel less scared now. Strange, that would have scared the hell out of me. But you are strong.

Together we have a purpose. *You see that now, right?*

As we practically fly onto a wider road—*freeway*—our hand slips unconsciously into a dark nook in the car's interior and comes out with a metal tin. It pops open, and we drop a small pellet into our mouth.

It explodes with flavor on our tongue.

Altoid. Mint.

I let you stretch our mouth out into a smile.

It's a flavor I'm unfamiliar with, but I can see that it has its charms. *A little like me'iorcha grass, maybe?*

It calms you a little, and that's good.

We zoom down the freeway toward the city. I can see it in the distance—a collection of stout multi-story buildings you call skyscrapers.

We laugh. These stacks of windows are tiny compared to the ey'alin that my people, the orn, created on our own world. Enormous, elegant structures of light and air that stretched into the red sky, challenging even the gods themselves in their heavenly kingdom.

I would spread my wings from my aerie and leap off of the balcony, feeling the sun hot on my leathery membranes, drinking in the warm morning air.

Gl'orn was a harsh world, but a beautiful one.

Until *He* came and stole our future.

I have been chasing *Him* ever since.

Red and blue lights flare up behind us, accompanied by a wailing howl. We tense up, our shoulder blades drawing together.

Authorities. *Police.* We were going too fast for your local regulations. *I don't have time for this.*

Dutifully we pull the car over on the side of the road.

The police officer pulls up behind us on a two-wheeled vehicle—a *motorcycle*—and strolls up to the car window.

We open it.

The police officer glares at me, looking like authorities everywhere. "License and registration."

We hit him hard with our fist.

He goes down in a pile on the roadway.

We start the car, ready to pull away, back onto the freeway. We must hurry now. There's no time left.

He'll die if you leave him there.

You found your voice, at last. It happens, sometimes.

We grunt. So will many more if we don't arrive in time.

You are insistent. Please don't let him die.

I admire that trait in you, even if it might cost you your world.

We sigh heavily.

I am not *that* person. I don't kill needlessly or without remorse. Still, time presses us forward.

We get out and haul the police officer's body away from the edge of the road as fast as we can, lying him down between his motorcycle and the brick wall. It's all we have time to do.

In seconds, we are on our way again.

Thank you.

We nod. I have not come so far, across so many worlds, that I have forgotten what I am fighting for. *Or who I am.* I will never be like *Him.*

I DON'T KNOW why I'm so chatty tonight. Nerves, I guess. Killing time. *Can't this car go any faster?*

I don't know how I first managed to slip through the transom to another world.

I came home early from work in the sti'rine mines and found *Him* in our bedroom, standing astride her.

His gleaming green knife in hand, his black wings spread in threat, her yellow ichor splattered across his chest like a war banner.

Aiaia was dead. My er'rech. My wife.

I threw myself at *Him*, knocking *Him* against the wall, and felt his surprise at my presence, my strength.

I wasn't supposed to be there.

And in that second, it flooded through me. What *He* was. Why *He* had come to my home. How *He* had just sealed the fate of my world by killing the one person who could have stopped what was coming.

I knew these things in an instant, burned into me like a brand by her death and his touch.

I stared at *Him*, my mouth opened in horror, feeling his knife as it sank into my own gut, reaching my hearts with expert precision.

The chaos-bringer had tried to wrench *himself* away, and when that failed, *He* fled in the only way *He* knew how.

Across the transom.

It was a golden light, a sudden rift in the air above Aiaia's body.

My body dying, I thrust my su'rrrah, my essence, after him. I followed *Him*, reaching out to *Him* instinctively, thrusting my very *self* after *Him* and leaving my dying mortal body behind.

It was the last time I saw her. Or our home.

I have chased *Him* across fifty worlds. Every time, I have failed to stop *Him*.

We slip off the freeway into *downtown* Sacramento.

You work here. You know the city well, including all of its streets and back ways.

Fate has chosen you to help me. Maybe this is the time I will end *Him*.

This part of town is marked mostly by residential units and short commercial buildings. It is a pretty enough city, not like the marvelous soaring white buildings of the Verills or the lush black garden parks of the Onri. But neat and tidy, filled with enormous trees that sway in the night breeze.

Regularly placed streetlamps light up the night, and residential windows glow golden with internal and reflected light.

He is getting closer. I can feel the pitch blackness of *His* soul.

Here, you can feel *Him* too.

You recoil—it's like touching hot acid. Maybe now you can understand better why I need you tonight.

If we fail, all is not lost, not right away. Your world will go on for a time. But there's a nexus coming, a stark choice to be made. And if *He* succeeds, she won't be there to make that choice.

Eventually your race will die, within the lifetime of your

children or your children's children. Your world as you knew it will be no more.

All of these things and places… trees, *Victorians*, people—men, women, and children. The natural world that nurtures you.

All of it will be gone.

You are *crying* inside. We're crying on the outside too. Water from our eyes. How it releases those rampaging emotions inside of us.

My Aiaia was a *beacon*. The light of the orn. Or she would have been, if she had lived. If she had the time to come to her potential.

Crying feels *right*.

I have reached a beacon before *Him* five times. And this early before *Him*—twice.

All of those times, I failed to stop *Him*.

One of these times, I will beat *Him* and kill *Him*—then this will be over.

We're here. We pull up against the curb, the car's *brakes* screeching. Blocking someone's *driveway*.

No matter. Your world's laws are nothing next to this. Your *life* is nothing next to this. Neither is mine.

Mine is already over. I just haven't accepted it yet, but I have nothing left to lose.

We leap out of the car and run up the steps of the squat two-story residence.

Bungalow.

Our lips quirk. It's a funny word.

We bang on the door.

Silence.

He draws rapidly closer, coming from the west. His presence brings up hives on our skin, our forearms rising in red welts.

His host is not as fast as mine. Or so I hope.

We bang on the door again.

A light comes on inside. "Who is it?" Her voice is strong, unafraid.

"Please, let me in. You're in danger. I'm here to help you." We try to sound calm, reasonable. Safe.

Her face appears at the window. Her skin is a few shades darker than ours. She is beautiful, like Aiaia. "Go away, or I'll call the police." She *is* scared.

Well, she *should* be. Just not of me.

We are becoming frantic. "There's no time. He's coming!" It is always like this—they never accept us right away.

She retreats, picking up something in the darkness of her room.

A *phone*.

We throw our weight against the door. Once, twice.

It rattles but does not give way.

A third time and it flies open, slamming into the wall behind it with a heavy crash, knocking several pictures off the wall.

She stands before us holding the phone, angry as she is frightened. "My name is Olivia Wells. Someone just broke into my home!" She backs away, reaching for something behind her as I approach.

She glows. Golden. Like the transom. We can see the light inside her. I was right. She is a beacon.

"Olivia, I'm not here to hurt you." We put our hands out, open palmed, in a way that you assure me is non threatening.

"Get out of my house, or I'll make you regret it." She's holding a long, pointed metal thing.

Fireplace poker.

He's here.

There is no more time.

We surge forward and put our hands on her face as she pushes the poker into our gut—a horrendously painful violation of pain and torn flesh.

We scream, but we hold on.

You scream inside me too. I block you out. And the pain, too. I must stay focused.

The light source—*lamp*—flickers and goes out.

The night is suddenly absolutely silent.

I can feel his presence, like a bloody tear in the fabric of the world. Like the gash in our stomach.

He is behind us.

Your life force seeps away with your ichor—*blood*—but I have enough time. Just enough time.

I slip from you through our hands, into her.

Olivia. I feel you screaming inside of us.

I am not here to hurt you. I open my heart and let Aiaia pour out of me into you. Everything she was to me. Everything I loved about her.

You feel it. Your scream trails off into a whimper. *You won't hurt me.*

No, Olivia. Never you. Only Him.

I feel your assent. You *are* strong, stronger than any I have ridden before.

We open our eyes. *He* stands before us.

It's dark in the room, but I know *Him.* Though wrapped in a plain unassuming package of human flesh, his eyes burn like coals, black as night, filled with the cold light of dying stars.

He raises his arm, holding the green knife *he* always carries with him.

I reach out to you. *You must trust me.* I feel your strength. Your resolve. You *know*. I don't know how, but you know what you are.

There's no time to marvel at it.

As *His* arm flashes down with the knife, we reach our arms out wide and *scream*.

Golden light blossoms in the room, flowing from us, bathing the chairs, the walls, and the floorboards where my last host lays in a pool of blood.

His wound stops bleeding, his skin stitching itself up.

The whole room ripples, and my nemesis howls as *He* begins to melt.

He screams at us, his darkness pushing back our light just a little.

We are stronger. Together we push back, and step by step against the howling wind, we force his black fire back into *Him*.

The curtains by the window flail about like the tentacles of an or'auch.

Bits of *Him* slip away, stripped off of *Him* like leaves in the wind—hair, fingernails, his ears.

His knife, held up in the air, glows red, then yellow, then white, and then the blade vanishes in a screech of dust, carried away on the wind of our voice.

The hilt clatters to the ground.

He loses form, blown away like black dust.

We push against him like the bitter vengeance of Fa'rad.

He reaches for us once more, *his* fingers sifting away into nothing as a dry howl comes out of *his* throat.

His eyes are the last to go, staring at us with bitter hatred and disgust.

Then *He* is gone in a cloud of dust. His host is gone too.

Poor soul.

The room plunges back into darkness.

The room's electric lights flicker back on, the lamp laying on its side on the wooden floor.

We kneel to pick up the hilt of his knife.

It's metal. *Silver*. Intricately cast with whorls and letters in some illegible language.

It glows in our palm, getting hot. Its blade growing again from the base to form a new knife. Golden this time, not green. Its knowledge passes into us.

There are more of them, like *Him*. I can feel *Them* now, all connected to him, part of a mission of chaos and disruption. The nameless ones. Someone must hunt them down.

I have more work to do before I go into ne'alia to find Aiaia's soul.

I am ready to give chase, but Olivia grasps me tight one last time. She opens up her su'rrrah to me, her very soul.

She is *Olivia*, *Aiaia*, and is a hundred others. A thousand. She is a *beacon*—all the beacons. They are connected, like the disruptors.

There are others like me out there too—the hunters.

All of us—disruptor, beacon, and hunter—are locked in a deadly dance of order vs. chaos.

I see it as clearly as I see the knife in our hand.

She lets me go.

The golden light of the transom beckons, opening for me alone now.

I blink in disbelief. I recognize the other side.

It's my home, undisturbed—before *He* came. The transoms cross not just space, but time as well.

I understand. They have given me another chance at life. I don't know how—I don't understand space-time or the transom, much less the byzantine twists of paradox.

I've done my part and ended one of the disrupters. If I choose, I can have a normal life again, with her. With Aiaia. The other hunters will carry on without me.

I slip away from Earth to Orn, back into my own aerie, back into my own body. I am a familiar host, yet strange now to myself.

Don't be afraid. I won't hurt you.

You recognize me, even though I am not who I was.

We nod and hide ourselves in the darkness, waiting for *Him* to come.

I no longer know what it is to be *normal.* I am bent and twisted by the chase—Aiaia would no longer recognize me.

We will save her.

Then we will continue the hunt.

JAMES WOKE. He was lying in a hospital bed. His stomach ached, but everything was fuzzy. "Kevin?"

His husband was at his side in an instant. "Hey, you okay?"

"I think so." He reached for his midsection. It felt whole. Sore, but not torn in two. He remembered gut-wrenching pain. *Was it all a dream?*

"Careful there. You took a fireplace poker to the stomach, though the doctor said it looked like it hardly nicked you. And that was after you punched a cop on the freeway and broke into some poor woman's house in midtown. What the hell happened on that walk?"

James shook his head. He remembered bits and pieces—racing down the highway. The stars shining above. Eyes black as night. But it was fuzzy, like a dream that slipped away when you awoke.

Something about saving the world? "I don't know. It's all a blur—"

Someone knocked at the door.

James turned to see who it was. Even that hurt. Then he stared at the woman who entered. He *knew* her. Somehow.

Kevin put himself between them. "You shouldn't be here, Olivia. Our lawyers will sort things out for us." Kevin put himself between James and the new arrival.

"I'm not pressing charges. He… clearly wasn't himself last night."

Kevin looked at her, then back at him.

"Look, I just want to see how he is. I come unarmed. There's no harm in it."

Kevin frowned. "I guess not?"

"It's okay, Kev." James felt no threat from this woman. He hoped she felt the same about him, after what he supposedly had done.

Kevin stepped aside, letting her pass.

"Just wanted to make sure you're okay." She sat on the edge of James's bed, putting a warm hand on his cheek. "Are you?"

It tingled where she touched him, and he felt instantly better, the pain seeping out of him like coffee through a filter.

James croaked. "I'm okay." The two of them had a connection. Something in common, though he couldn't quite put his finger on it. Something had happened the night before. Olivia was a *beacon*. Someone had told him so.

Olivia smiled at him, and for a moment he thought she was glowing.

He shook his head. Those must be some damned good pain meds.

She was here. And alive.

Somehow, he knew that meant everything was going to be right. "I'm a little tired."

Kevin kissed his forehead, and Olivia squeezed his hand.

"Go to sleep. We'll work things out when you're feeling better." Kevin exuded warmth, love, safety.

James nodded, grateful. *Later sounds good.*

He closed his eyes and fell asleep, dreaming of gossamer buildings that reached halfway to space under a hot red sky.

About Across the Transom

I LITERALLY WOKE up at two in the morning with this story in my head. Most of my story ideas come during my waking hours, but for this one, I got up and wrote it right then, in one sitting.

And unlike most things I scribble down in the middle of the night, I could actually read it (and it wasn't half bad!).

PAREIDOLIA

Simon slammed the lid on his sugar-free, two-pump, pulse-heated vanilla latte, before he might accidentally get a good look at the pattern on the coffee's surface.

Ethan, the barista, usually covered it for him, but he'd forgotten this time. Simon, distracted by the coffee shop's textured wall, had almost missed it.

He'd jerked his gaze away when the whorls and lines in the plaster had shifted into a mountain landscape. He looked around as casually as he could manage, hoping no one had noticed the wall moving.

Simon put his prescription glasses back on. They blurred his vision just enough to block his curse from shifting any other patterns. If anyone ever found out what he could do, they'd stick him in a cage like a lab rat.

Fooling the optometrist had been easy enough—he'd just pretended that the clear letters were fuzzy and vice versa. Unfortunately, they made the handsome barista fuzzy too.

Simon sighed under his breath. An imperfect solution to an unwanted gift. He waved. "Have a good one."

"You too." Ethan winked at him.

Simon hurried out of the Student Union, keeping his eyes pointed forward, avoiding the patterns that flocked to him like birds to seed—clouds in the sky, the grains of wood on a table… even the swirls on Tracey Martin's designer bag in class. He emerged into the fresh morning air, ducking as a drone zipped past overhead carrying a pizza to someone's dorm.

He'd learned to control his curse in elementary school. *Mostly.* The glasses helped, and if he blurred his vision when the patterns started to become *actual things*, they stopped. Usually. Still, he'd gone to detention more than once for, "whatever you just did to your desk."

There was a name for seeing things in random patterns—pareidolia. But most people didn't seem to do it so literally.

"Ally, what's the time?"

His PA responded in his ear in her usual chipper Italian accent. *-It's eleven-fifty-seven, Simon. You have a class in three minutes.-*

"Crap." He ran down the steps, knocking the wallet out of a woman's hands. He grabbed it and tossed it to her. "Sorry!"

Then he bolted down the sidewalk, dodging a group of students flicking data over their wrists, and leapt like a track star over a short hedge to shave off fifteen seconds.

One of the Sac State professors shouted after him, "Slow down!"

"Sorry! Late for a lecture!" He hated being late—it drew attention to himself, and he liked to blend in. *Plus, it's a damned good course.*

Professor Dandrich's course—*Finding Meaning in Interstellar Noise*—was one of his favorites. If he could just find a job like that where he could use his strange ability…

Simon slipped into the hall and slammed into his seat in the front row of the lecture hall at a minute past noon, splashing his latte all over his arm. "Dammit."

Everyone turned to look at him, and heat rushed to his face. *So much for blending in.*

"Nice of you to join us, Mr. Walker." Professor Dandrich was six-foot-two and thin as a bird, with long blond hair that Simon sometimes imagined was feathers. He'd even started to change it, once, before he caught himself and looked away.

She handed him a Kleenex and went back to addressing the class.

"Ally, record," he said under his breath.

"So, we were discussing Fermi's Paradox. There *should* be life everywhere out there. Why don't we see any signs of it?" She waved at the sky through the open windows.

"Because the aliens know we're a race of fucked-up assholes?" Jacob Hines, the redneck class clown, grinned at his own joke. The rest of the class laughed.

Professor Dandrich didn't rise to the bait. "That's one theory. Any others?"

Next to him, Tiana Jones brushed one of her braided locks behind her ear and raised her hand. "Maybe once you reach sentience and discover carbon, you can't help but turn your world into a global hothouse?"

Professor Dandrich nodded. "Better. Someone's been paying attention."

Tiana grinned.

The Professor paced slowly back and forth across the dais, flicks of her hand bringing images up on the large screen before them. Factories. Oil derricks. Solar panel arrays and wind farms. "We can guess that intelligent life takes a long time to develop, which would allow for the creation of reserves of oil, coal, and natural gas over millions or even billions of years. But wouldn't some of them evolve out of it?"

Danny Meeker jumped in. "What about nuclear war?"

"Sure. That would knock out a few more." A nuclear cloud loomed over the class.

Simon raised his own hand. "What if we're just looking *wrong*?"

That got him a smile. The screen went blank, brightening the room. "How'd you arrive at that idea, Mr. Walker?"

He grinned. "Well, it's implied in the name of the course."

Professor Dandrich's eyebrow lifted. "You're smarter than you look, behind that mild-mannered façade." She turned to the rest of the class. "So what do we think of Mr. Walker's idea?"

The discussion devolved into a pitched back and forth over dead aliens vs. avoidance of Earth by discerning ones.

His mind drifted—the glasses kept the world around him at a safe distance, but also made it easier to become distracted.

Five-year-old Simon lay on his stomach on a frayed tan and brown carpet. He was wearing his favorite black shirt and red shorts, his legs flopping back and forth in the air behind him. He stared at the patterns in the rug, his eyes narrowing, and tried to make pictures out of them.

Above him, Mamma talked to the doctor, a nice young man in a white coat with a tablet in his hand.

"...there *are* no more tests, Mrs. Walker. There's nothing wrong with him."

The words floated on the surface of his mind like leaves on a pond and then fluttered away as if blown by a sharp breeze.

"There *is* something wrong with him. Look at him."

In the rug's pattern, Simon found a giraffe, tracing its outline with his finger. It turned to stare at him, placidly chewing on a branch it had broken off the tree he'd traced a moment before.

"My friend Mona said he was probably autistic. Or... what's that other one? Something with 'burgers' in it?"

A werewolf had joined the giraffe, stalking it from the long grass, its teeth bared.

"Your son does not have *Aspergers*, Mrs. Walker. Some first-graders are just a little slower to develop social skills and awareness."

"It's the *vaccines*, isn't it? Mona told me not to give them to him. But the school nurse insisted—"

There. He could *see* the wall between the giraffe and the werewolf, too tall for it to climb. Simon liked giraffes. Werewolves, not so much.

"There's no known link between vaccines and autism, Mrs. Walker. And I don't think Simon's autistic. He's just... some kids are less social than others."

Simon's mother ruffled his hair.

Simon looked up at her. "Is it lunch time yet? I'm hungry."

She flashed him a worried smile. "Are you sure?"

"Let's just wait and see how things go over the next couple months. We can revisit it next time. In the meantime, why don't you set up some play dates with other kids about Simon's age?"

Simon frowned. He didn't like other kids very much.

He looked down—the giraffe and the werewolf were gone. In their place was a muddy blur, as if the colors of the carpet had all run together.

His mother didn't notice. She *never* did.

"Thank you, Doctor Quan. I'll... we'll call you in a month or two for another appointment." She reached down and took Simon's hand and pulled him toward the door.

The doctor's voice floated after them. "Jenn, something happened to the carpet. Can you come take a look?"

They slipped out of the waiting room and into the warm afternoon sunlight.

Simon looked up at the sky and smiled. His giraffe cavorted in the clouds above, safe from all predators.

SOMEONE TOUCHED HIS SHOULDER.

Simon started, looking up into Professor Dandrich's brown eyes. She was *really* tall. Her red cardigan was pulled tightly to her chest under her crossed arms.

The room was silent. He looked around—the rest of the class had already left. "Sorry. I… got distracted."

She nodded, leaning against the long desktop in front of him. "That seems to be happening a lot lately. Are you getting enough sleep?"

"Not really." He was taking thirty credits this semester—ten classes kept him too busy to get into trouble. "I have a lot on my plate."

She frowned, reaching out to him "Can I see your glasses?"

"What?" He looked up at her, his brow creased. "I… don't really feel comfortable taking them off." His anxiety edged up, a cold sweat breaking out on his forehead.

"Please indulge me." Her voice was kind but firm.

Simon didn't see a way out, other than fleeing the class and being too embarrassed to return. And he *liked* this class. He sighed. *I can control it. For a couple minutes.*

He pulled them off and handed them over. He looked straight ahead, blurring his vision, trying not to actually *see* anything.

She held them up to the light, frowning. "I think these might be the wrong prescription." She set them down on his desk. "Look at me, Simon." Her voice was gentle but brooked no argument.

He looked at her face. *That* was safe enough. It didn't *work* on animate things.

"How many fingers am I holding up?"

"Two," he said without thinking.

She brushed a stray lock of her blond hair behind her ear. "Don't lie to me."

Simon sighed. "Four."

A sly smile slid across her face. "So, you *can* see clearly without these. At this prescription, you should be blind as a bat without them."

"Yes, ma'am." His mother had always taught him to be polite.

"So why do you wear them? They must give you terrible headaches."

"They used to." His hand flew up to cover his mouth. "Really, I'd rather not say."

She stared at him for a moment, then nodded. "Fair enough." She swiped her wrist, bringing up her calendar in midair. "I'd like to see you during office hours tomorrow. Can you manage one o'clock?"

"I… sure. Am I in trouble?" All those times in the principal's office in high school flashed before his eyes.

"No, not at all." Her gaze softened, and for just a second she reminded him of his mother. "I just want to help you." She flicked her wrist, and a faint whooshing sound announced the sending of her message. "Okay, added. Please send me a confirmation when you get it. See you tomorrow!"

SIMON STARTED TO KNOCK, then held back, his hand hovering in midair. He had a *bad* feeling about this. He'd mostly managed to avoid direct contact with his professors outside class, up to this point. Why break a winning streak? *I should go.*

"Come in, Simon." Professor Dandrich's voice startled him.

He sighed and opened the heavy, old metal door and entered her office. He stopped short, surprised by the difference—inside, it was light and airy, with floor-to-ceiling windows looking out on a sunny courtyard. A pleasing medley of bushes—red photinia, green ferns, and sage-gray lavender—surrounded a tall redwood tree, screening off most of the brick wall of the next building.

Professor Dandrich's desk was glass, neat, and clear of clutter.

She stood and offered her hand, shaking his. "Thanks for coming, Simon. Have a seat, please."

He sank down into the comfortable leather chair, wary of what was coming next. "Professor Dandrich—"

She smiled. "Please, call me Candace."

"Okay… Candace." Simon frowned. *That feels… weird.* "Why am I here? I'm sorry about nodding off in class yesterday. I was just really tired—" He had a whole litany of excuses collected from years of explaining away his curse.

"Don't worry, Simon. You're not in trouble." She turned to her laptop screen and her eyes narrowed. "I've been doing a bit of looking into your… situation." She looked up at him, her eyes full of something. Compassion? Pity? Curiosity?

Simon couldn't tell.

"I think you've been keeping a secret for a really long time, and it's wearing you down."

His eyes widened. "What do you mean? I don't have any secrets, Professor Dandrich. I'm just Simon."

"Candace. And I think you know exactly what I'm talking about, Simon."

He pushed his glasses back up on his nose, his heart beating fast. "I really don't." He wished he were anywhere but in her office.

Candace leaned forward on her desk, clasping her hands, and looked him right in the eye. "You can see things that others miss. Your mind makes connections between bits of random visual information."

"I don't know—"

"You see things in patterns that no one else sees. Am I right?"

He shrugged, struggling to keep his voice even. "I… sometimes. It's called pareidolia. Everyone does it."

A slow grin slid across her face. "Do you know how many other students in your class know that word? I'd bet not a one." She shook her head. "And you're wrong. Everyone *thinks* they see things in random patterns. I saw a dragon in the clouds the other day, breathing fire across the heavens. I took a picture of it and shared it with one of my colleagues, and *she* saw Albert Einstein." She snorted. "You're right. Everyone does *that*. But I think you can do more." She opened a desk drawer and pulled out a piece of shiny photo paper and slid it across the desk. "Tell me what *you* see."

Simon looked at it. It was a fuzzy blue-and-white image. "Not much? Clouds?"

"Take off your glasses."

His stomach twisted. "I really don't think…"

She put her hand on his. It was warm. "Please, Simon. You can trust me. I won't tell anyone else." Her lips quirked. "Keeping this inside has been hard on you, hasn't it? Wouldn't it be easier to share it with someone else?" Something about the way she said it got to him. Like, she *really* needed him to. Like there were lives depending on it.

He sighed, pulling away. "Okay. But you won't tell anyone else?"

"Scout's honor."

His hand shook as he took off his glasses and set them on the desk. Before he could second-guess himself, he ripped the metaphorical Band-Aid off, picking up the paper and staring at the image.

There was nothing at first, just a bunch of clouds in a blue sky.

Then his mind saw it—a dragon prowling across the page in search of a knight to eat.

As he stared at it, the outlines firmed up. Sharp white teeth grew at the sides of its mouth, and the fire from its mouth turned from white to orange. Its eyes came alive, and it glared at him.

He threw it down as if the paper had burned him and pulled his glasses back on hurriedly. "I'm sorry."

Candace picked up the image. Her mouth dropped open as she stared at it. "That's... impressive." She bit her lip as her fingers traced the outlines of the fearsome creature. "Seems I was right about you."

Simon waited for the inevitable explosion of anger or disbelief, maybe even fear.

Instead, she simply nodded and smiled. "Thank you, Simon. That was very brave." She put the picture away in a desk drawer. "You're wasting your time here at Sac State. What you can do..." She took his hand again. "Simon, you're special."

"Short bus special?"

She laughed. "No, the other kind. We've only found a handful of others with similar abilities."

He stared at her, not believing what he'd just heard. "There are others like me?"

"Oh yes. We've been watching you for a long time, but you aren't the only one." She squeezed his hand. "Would you like to meet them?"

Simon couldn't believe it. He wasn't *alone*. There were other people just like him, out there in the world. He grinned, an unaccustomed feeling coursing through him. Happiness. "Yes, please."

She nodded. "Do you have any classes this afternoon?"

"Just one." Professor Millar's statistics course was a snoozer—he could afford to skip a week. "Where are we going?"

It was a good hour and a half from Sacramento to Orinda. Simon and his mother had stopped in the small foothills community east of San Francisco for gas once, when he was in Junior High, on the way to the City for yet another medical consultation. He remembered nothing about that trip besides the town's iconic art deco theater, the marquee towering over him against a clear blue sky.

On the way, Professor Dandrich—Candace, which was still *weird*—tried to make casual conversation with him, but Simon responded in single word answers, and soon she gave up and left him alone.

I need time to think. Simon stared at the parchment-yellow hills as they slipped past the window—empty save for the occasional tree or bush or grazing cow, their rippling patterns too far away and moving too fast for his curse to affect.

He tried to wrap his head around the idea of being around others like himself, of no longer having to hide who he was and what he could do. What would they be like? Were they near his age? Younger? Way older… like thirty?

He was a college kid. *I should be having the time of my life.* Wild parties, experimenting with his classmates. But even sex was forbidden to him by his curse.

Zach fumbled with the door handle. "Roomie's in physics for another hour, so the dorm's all ours."

Simon swallowed and nodded, pulse racing and filled with *need*, unable to respond rationally. "Okay." He'd been wanting this for weeks, watching Zach like some love-struck idiot.

His heart pounded in his chest and he broke out in a cold sweat.

He glanced up and down the dorm hallway. They were all alone.

He grabbed Zach by the shirt and turned him around, kissing him hungrily. It was springtime, and he'd been hibernating all winter in his room with a box of Kleenex and a bottle of lube.

Zach responded with fervor.

The door burst inward, spilling them into Zach's dorm room and onto his bed.

"Do you have any—"

"Oh, yeah." Zach sank down on the bed and pulled off his white shirt, throwing it on the floor. He pulled open his nightstand drawer, filled with candy-colored condom wrappers.

Simon shrugged out of his own shirt. He'd fooled around in high school with limited success, but this… Zach was beautiful, his swimmer physique a heady drug that promised to scratch Simon's itch.

And his boxers…

Simon stared, transfixed, as the blue and gold paisley pattern on Zach's underwear shifted, twisting into ocean waves, rising and falling as they swept around Zach's waist.

Zach's gaze followed his own, his green eyes settling on his crotch.

"What the fuck?" He scrambled back across the bed, away from Simon, trying to pull off his shorts—for all the wrong reasons.

Simon turned beet red, his face on fire. "I'm sorry…"

"You did this?" Zach was naked, holding his boxers at arm's length.

Simon didn't know where to look. "I'm sorry!" It came out in an anguished cry. He grabbed his shirt and ran out of the room and down the hall, his face hot with shame.

"SIMON?"

Simon blinked—sun was shining in his eyes through the windshield. Rumors had circulated after that incident, but no one believed Zach, so they'd died down eventually. Still, he heard the whispers. *Strange Simon.*

"We're here." Candace pulled her Chevy Zip into a space along a quiet sidewalk.

Simon sat up and looked out the window, up at that old movie theater marquee on an art deco-style building—the same one he'd seen as a kid. "Um… okay. This is it?"

"Yup." She grabbed her briefcase from the back. "Come on. I'll introduce you to the others."

"Sure." He climbed out of the car to look around. It was a cute little downtown, emphasis on "little"—nestled among grass- and oak-covered hills. It had clean sidewalks, terra-cotta pots filled with flowers, and little shops with striped awnings—someone's idea of small-town perfection.

On the next corner, a local market's produce stands held huge watermelons, striped Tuscan cantaloupes and bright red apples.

Not what I expected. Not that he was at all sure what he *did* expect—maybe a secret underground lair, or a penthouse superhero's apartment filled with gadgets, support geeks, and eight-foot-wide video screens?

But not *this* suburban daydream.

Candace swiped her wrist across the meter's screen to pay, getting a beep in response. "God, I hate parking meters." She pulled out a set of metal keys to unlock the theater doors.

Simon grabbed his milkshake from the center console, and his backpack from the back seat, and followed her inside.

The lobby looked abandoned, full of dust and candy wrappers and fading old posters for films like Birds of Prey, The Assistant and Sonic the Hedgehog. "What is this place?"

"It was great little theater in its day. Just three screens—not the twenty-plexes we have now—each in a different theme. One's hardly bigger than a living room. That's the dorm." She waved her wrist over a glass pad by a suspiciously new looking door at the back—a heavy, metal beast of a thing. It swung open silently, revealing a long hall with a light at the back. "Unfortunately, it didn't survive. Come on."

Simon nodded. He remembered that year of home schooling. He'd actually enjoyed being at home, unlike some of his peers.

The door closed behind them with a soft *thunk*.

Just down the hall, she opened a side door and ushered him inside.

Simon stepped into wonderland.

Floor-to-ceiling art déco murals covered the walls, including lush paintings of gorgeous idealized, shirtless, chiseled men. Turquoise and purple lights lit the ceiling, and there actually *were* eight-foot monitors—three of them—lined up on the stage in front of the old theater screen. Two young women—twins, by the look of them—stood before them, staring at swirling patterns and murmuring.

Welcome to the mad scientist's lair. Simon grinned.

Below the stage, a wide, round white table held some sort of three-dimensional image—a hologram—that also swirled with strange patterns. He was dying to take off his glasses and get a better look. Three others, all about his age, were staring at the image.

The rest of the room was filled with gadgets that would have made that mad scientist cream his pants—Rube Goldberg machines that twisted and turned and shifted to no apparent purpose.

Candace cleared her throat. "Everyone, we have a visitor. This is Simon."

"Hey Simon!" The twins were taller than him, and thin as a rail. The one who spoke had her dark hair pulled back in corn rows, while the other's was short and frizzy. "We're Tawnea and Dorrence. *She her hers.*"

"I'm Jacin, and these are Todd and Coryn." Jacin was tall, blond, blue-eyed, lithe like a swimmer. *Just my type.* Simon tried not to stare. "Todd and I use *he him his*, while Coryn here is *they them theirs.*"

Todd was half Jacin's size, a little person with a shock of dark hair and a grin as wide as his face, wearing a backwards blue baseball cap. "Nice to meet you." He held out his hand.

Simon shook it, liking him immediately. "You're…"

"Better looking than you expected? I get that a lot." His grin got even wider, if that was even possible.

Simon laughed. "I was going to say *really friendly*. But let's go with that."

Coryn's dark hair was cropped short, their arched eyebrow promising *mischief.*

Simon looked around. "So what is this place?"

"This is the Platform for the Activation of Transitory Talents Emergent in Random Networks." Coryn nodded seriously.

Simon's eyes must have gone wide, because Coryn laughed. "We just call it the Pattern Patch." The others joined in, cackling and chuckling, their laughter filling the room.

That laughter echoed in his head, bring back all the others who had mocked him before. His stomach twisted. *Strange Simon.* Those dark eyes taunted him. *Strange Simon, strange Simon, strange Simon!*

"Sorry, I just… I can't." Simon ran out of the room, his face flushed. The empty hallway flashed by, but the hulking metal door blocked his path. He pushed on it, then tried slamming his shoulder into it, but it wouldn't open. "Fuck."

"That won't work, you know." Candace's voice was light, but she sounded worried for him. "It's restricted access, and that door is five times your weight."

"So I'm a prisoner here?" He turned to face her, his stomach in knots. *Why did I come?* He could have stayed at Sac State if he wanted people to laugh at him and look at him funny.

Candace shook her head. "No, not at all. If you don't want to stay, you can go. I'll take you back to your dorm tonight." She looked at him the way few people ever did, with no judgment. "Hear me out first?"

"I… guess." He could manage that much.

"Come back in. Coryn didn't mean anything. They just get a bit over excited when we get someone new." She held out her hand.

He looked at it for a moment, then took it. *What's the harm?* He let her lead him back down the hall and through the laboratory.

Coryn looked up as they reentered the room. "Sorry, Simon." They flashed him a brief smile. "I didn't mean to scare you off."

Todd raised his arms menacingly and growled. "That's my job."

Simon cracked a smile and nodded. "It's okay. I'm just a little sensitive right now. This is all so new."

Coryn squeezed his shoulder. "It freaked me out a little, too."

"Come on. I have something to show you." Candace winked at him. "The rest of you get back to work."

"What, a secret chamber?" *There's always a secret chamber.* A little of his excitement crept back in.

"You'll see." Candace flashed him a mysterious grin.

He followed her to a small door at the back of the cavernous room and looked back at the others. They'd gone back to whatever they'd been working on, though Todd shot him a thumbs-up.

He went through the door after Candace.

A narrow stair led into darkness, down new-looking cement steps. The walls were unfinished drywall, and whoever had put them in hadn't even bothered to paint the plain gray surface.

Round LED bulbs hung at regular intervals and came on one at a time as they followed the stairway down into the Earth. "PATTERN, huh?"

Candace laughed. "That's just Coryn being Coryn. They have a warped sense of humor."

Simon wanted to like Coryn. He really did. "Did the theater have a basement?"

"Not originally." Candace looked up at him over her shoulder, smiling cryptically.

Simon grinned. "So, there is a secret lair."

"Something like that."

Simon counted at least a hundred steps on the way down. His thighs ached by the time they reached the bottom.

They reached the bottom and stepped out into an irregular cavern. What he could see in the dim light looked natural, save for the leveled concrete floor—the same material that made up the stairs.

"What is this place?" He wished he could get a better look without his glasses.

"The theater closed last year. They hit a rough patch after the Great Pause, when everyone was watching movies on streaming. The government bought it through a shell corporation and put out a cover story about using it as a theater school. They chose it, in part, because of easy access to this space." She palmed a switch on the wall, and lights came up, illuminating a natural cavern.

Simon looked around. The cave's walls were encrusted with stalactites and stalagmites that swirled like melted candle wax, sometimes touching to form columns. Darkness on one side indicated a possible exit. The air was still and warm.

In the center of the room, something was covered in a black cloth.

Simon crossed his arms. "So, go ahead, give me your spiel."

Candace nodded. "Come here." She put her hands on his shoulders and steered him gently to stand in front of the hidden thing. "Whatever happens, whatever you decide, I want you to swear to me you won't disclose what you see in this room, or in this facility."

Simon frowned. "That sounds ominous."

"It is. I work for the Department of Defense, and they know how to disappear people. You don't want to end up in some place like Guantanamo."

He stared at her, not sure if she was being serious, but this time she didn't smile. "Okay. My lips are sealed."

She nodded. "Just say your name and swear it." She held her wrist up to record him.

He snorted. "I swear."

"Say 'I, Simon Walker, swear not to disclose what I see in this place.'"

He held up his hand like he'd seen on TV. "I, Simon Walker, swear not to disclose what I see in this place."

She saved the file with a few swipes over her wrist, and then nodded. "Okay. You ready?"

Simon took a deep breath, his hands trembling. This suddenly felt deadly serious. "I think so?"

Candace pulled off the cloth.

There was a plastic crate with DARPA printed on the side, and on top of it, a strange, curved white object. It was about the size of a large watermelon, covered with whorls and converging and diverging lines. Simon's his glasses wouldn't let him make them out too closely. "So… that's it? A piece of art?"

Candace stared at him, her brow furrowing. "Take off your glasses."

He hesitated. He felt naked anymore, without them.

"Please."

Simon bit his tongue. He'd come all this way for this. With a sigh, he pulled them off.

At once the spirals and lines on the object moved, surging around like little waves. And it wasn't exactly white, either. If he looked closely, he could see whorls of green and blue and purple and red, tucked into the glowing brilliance of the thing.

It was like nothing he'd ever seen before.

It reacted to him as if it *knew* he was there. It was mesmerizing. The lines formed and merged, reminding him of nothing so much as the clouds of Jupiter in a time lapse video.

Something about it called to him. Without thinking, he reached out to touch it. A shock of electricity ran up his arm, knocking him back against the cavern wall and into darkness.

SOMEONE PATTED his face with a cold cloth. Simon opened his eyes.

Coryn was staring down at him, their brow furrowed.

They were squinting at him. "You okay? Candace says you touched at the Egg and it knocked you out."

"The egg?"

Coryn nodded. "Capital 'E.' They found it the day we were all born." They grinned. "It's cool, isn't it?"

"Yeah, I suppose." Simon didn't want to admit the magnetic pull it had over him. He sat up and swung his legs off the edge of the mattress, looking around. They were in a long, narrow room that looked like nothing so much as an ancient Pharaoh's tomb, decorated in garish blues and golds—probably part of the original theater's decor. He grinned. *They loved bright and gaudy, didn't they?*

Metal bunk beds had been mounted to the walls, and the floor sloped up noticeably from one side to the other. "Where am I?"

"This is the dorm. Tawny and Dorry carried you up here after you fainted." Coryn leaned in. "Did the Egg *move*? Candace said it moved." They sounded excited.

"The lines on it moved, yeah." He wondered if the others could do what he did—make real things appear out of random patterns.

"Well, that's new." Cory turned toward the open door. "Hey guys, he's awake!"

Tawny poked her head inside. "You feel okay?" She sounded concerned.

Simon blushed. "Yeah, I just fell. Nothing broken." He realized he wasn't wearing his glasses.

"Good. I'll get Candace." She popped back out again.

"Looking for these?" Coryn handed him his glasses.

"Yeah, thanks." He put them on, but the lenses were cracked.

"I think you fell on them. Can you see okay without them?"

"Yeah. Well enough." *A little too well.* Simon sighed. Then something struck him. "You said 'the day we were all born'?"

"Yes. December 17th, 2005. That's your birthday too, right?"

"Yeah… but I don't understand. What does that have to do with anything?"

Coryn nodded. "None of us knew, at first. Candace will fill you in. We think you're the last one."

"The last one?" *What the heck have I gotten into?*

Coryn got up and ambled over to a small white refrigerator in the corner. "Here, drink this." He tossed Simon a plastic container filled with a brown liquid.

Simon stared at it suspiciously. "What is it? Truth serum?"

Coryn laughed. "Hardly. Just chocolate milk. My own recipe—twice as much chocolate and a bit of vanilla extract. It helps calm my nerves when I'm worried."

Simon opened it and sipped the cold liquid. It tasted *amazing*. "Thanks, Coryn."

"Call me Cory." They grinned and sipped on another bottle. "Candace will explain everything."

As if summoned, the professor arrived at the doorway, followed by the others. "Hey Simon, you feeling a little better?"

Coryn nodded. "He has questions."

"Like we all did when we came here." Jacin sat next to him and held out his hand.

Simon stared at it for a moment, then took it. "Thanks, Jacin."

Something electric passed between them, and Simon felt warm inside. Something about him felt familiar. "Call me Jace."

Simon grinned. Maybe these *others* weren't so bad, after all.

Candace pulled up a chair and sat in front of him, pulling his attention away from the beautiful man holding his hand. "Of course you do. Ask away."

He nodded. "Coryn said we were all born on the same day." He wasn't sure how to ask the next part. "Do they all have my… talent?" He'd always thought of it as more of a curse.

"Yes, to some extent. You all have an affinity for patterns. Each one manifests it a little differently." She waved at the twins. "Tawny and Dorry can find hidden messages and connections in them. Todd and Jace can create images in midair. Cory… well, we're not quite sure what Cory can do yet, but they seem to amplify the others. But no one can manipulate patterns like you can."

Simon looked at the others.

They all nodded in unison.

"That's fire." Jacin squeezed his hand.

"Cory said I was the last one. Last one of what?"

"The *travelers*. We've been searching for you for years. You were really hard to find—born off the grid, apparently."

Travelers? Simon blushed. "Yeah. my mom was living in a compound in Utah when I was born. She left soon after. I don't remember it."

She tousled his hair, reminding him so much of his mother it gave him a lump in his throat. He should call her, tell her where he was.

"Come back to the laboratory. The others have something to show you." She held out a hand and pulled him up from the bed and led him out of the dorm to the vast room where he'd first met the others.

Simon looked around, trying to imagine what the place had been like as a movie theater.

The big round table dominated the middle of the space. It had a raised white bar that ran around the outer edge, and there were six seats spaced evenly around it.

Tawny and Dorry took two—side by side, naturally. Todd and Coryn were next—Todd's raised with a little button on the side. "Cool, right?"

Simon nodded and grinned.

Each of them put their hands on the bar, and a shaky, fuzzy image formed above the table.

Jace took a seat and added his palms.

The image steadied. It was a round room of some sort, like the Enterprise bridge—shiny and sleek and high-tech. There were… beings seated around the room. But they were fuzzy too. Not fuzzy in resolution. Fuzzy in conception. But how he knew that, he couldn't say. "What is it?"

"The table? Or the scene?" Candace put a hand on his shoulder.

"The table. The scene. Both." Simon frowned.

"The table's an imager." Coryn grinned. "We built it to let us use our abilities together. To *remember*."

"So that's... a memory?" *What, are they all secretly cosplay nuts?*

Todd held out a hand. "Sit down and find out."

Simon frowned. *I've come this far...* He took the seat next to Jace. "Now what?"

"Put your hands here." Jace guided him, his touch sending shock waves up Simon's arm.

Simon adjusted his jeans. "Okay, now what do I—" His hands contacted the imager, and the world *shifted.*

IMNYL WAS ON THE BRIDGE. It was blindingly white, patterns crawling over every surface, glowing with multi-colored light, just like the Egg.

The ship shuddered as it plunged through the outer layers of the atmosphere.

Imnyl could feel Jlemm behind him, staring over his—shoulder? Whatever that bony protrusion was. He was a nightmare of weird angles that shifted without warning, like the rest of his team. -*What's happening?*- The query came out in flashes of light.

Imnyl shifted, expressing his reply. -*We came out too close to the planet. We're trapped in its gravitational well. I'm trying to flatten our trajectory to skip us out, but...*-

The ship groaned. Flames licked her as she shot into the atmosphere, turbulence almost knocking him out of his chair.

Next to him, Slyrn and Mllni, the pattern hunters, were flying madly through different configurations, searching for something to save the ship with their pointed three-fingered hands. Colors flickered above their consoles, weaving together and flying apart like the feathers of a zynta bird.

Nimmh, one of the pattern spinners, spun an image of their destination, a series of grass-covered hills near a wide blue bay.

Coryn stood at his side, boosting him.

-I can't do it.- Imnyl fought the ship, but gravity was its own mistress, pulling them down to certain destruction. *We have to—*

Jlemm nodded, his eyes solemn above his forked nose. Still, he flickered in distress, his body shifting from form to form. *-We knew something bad might happen. They can re-gen our bodies.-*

-If *they find us.-* They locked eyes. *-Are you sure?-* He and Jlemm had been *scylall* for years—they knew each other intimately, and their patterns fit together like one.

Rescue might come soon, or never. Scouting missions were always high risk.

Jlemm brushed his fingers along the soft slits of Imnyl's neck, a gesture so intimate that the others all turned away, even in the midst of urgent chaos. Understanding passed between them in an instant. *-Yes, Imnyl. Do it.-*

Imnyl flashed his assent and turned back to his station. He sent the emergency sequence, and a pattern sprang up in the air in front of him, a weft of the fabric of space-time within the confines of the bridge. He stared at it and reality shifted, flooding off the screen and into the ship herself, which began to dissolve around them.

The others touched hands, creating a feedback circuit for him to work with and changing the pattern. The weft shifted and roared into them, ripping them to pieces.

Imnyl screamed, his bond with Jlemm buffering the worst of the pain as the shifting, coruscating light of the pattern devoured their own and transformed them and the ship into something new. It ripped him apart and then the pain was no more.

A strange, glowing meteor, harder than diamond, slammed into the idyllic hills, sending up a cloud of dust and rocks and grass and trees into the air to deposit microscopic bits of them for miles all around.

THE WORLD WENT DARK, but Imnyl/Simon's eyes didn't open. He was trapped in a blank netherworld, alone and afraid. He was empty, patternless, a neutral entity in a blank space, and he'd never felt more alone or afraid. "Hello?"

Then something touched his hand.

Impulses raced up his nerves, his arm forming from the vast nothing. Slowly the rest of him reappeared.

He had form again, his body emerging from the void. Relief washed through him, chasing away the fear.

Another hand squeezed his. It was Jace's hand, the skin hot in his own.

Jlemm.

-We were scylall once.-

-Yes.- Warmth surged through the bond, and understanding. *Scylall.* Soulmates. But it was a bond far deeper than Simon had ever understood.

Their patterns continued to twist around one another, weaving themselves back together.

Through his bond with Jace, Simon could feel Coryn, and through Coryn, Todd and Dorry and Tawny.

The pattern rippled through their circuit, bringing memories with it—recollections big and small, of another life lived in another form, in another place under a bright green sun. *Trillyn.* The name struck him with the force of a sledgehammer.

The place where he and Jlemm/Jace had been lovers, against the backdrop of an age of expansion and exploration, as the *elymm* had ventured beyond their own world to claim the stars.

Long ago, when he had been young and brave and foolish. Simon grinned. *Some things never change.*

He felt Jace's agreement through the bond.

These *travelers*, as Candace called them, weren't strangers. He saw that now. -*You're my family.*- Warmth filled him again, and recognition.

Simon opened his eyes. The light of the room seemed dim and sad after that bright bridge. "How… long ago?"

Jace's green eyes met his. "A couple hundred thousand years."

Simon bit his lip. The memories were so fresh. His litter mates, his four parents, his entire world. All long gone now. Trillyn—heart of the Three Hundred Worlds—might still exist out there, but it would be irrevocably changed by now.

Still… isn't that where I belong? He wasn't human. Not really.

"You okay?" Candace squeezed his shoulders from behind.

"Yeah. No. I mean… how am I supposed to answer that?" *I just found out I'm an interstellar freak.* "Why now? Why am I here, in this body?" He turned to look at her.

"A couple from Sac State was exploring these caverns after the '89 quake exposed an entrance to them here in the foothills. In 2005, they found the cathedral I took you to, and the Egg. When they tried to move it, something happened which knocked them out. When they woke up—"

"Something like what?" He

"We didn't know at first. DARPA took over the site to study the Egg, but it resisted all of our attempts to move it or break into it. It confounded every scan we could think to run on it." She leaned against the table, her eyes fixed on his. "Then we started getting reports of local kids with strange abilities. *Quirks*, they called them at first. There were a few reports in local papers before we shut it down. People find it easier to believe in a hoax than in the reality right in front of them." She flashed him a wry smile.

"They put together a task force and soon discovered that all the kids had been born on the same day."

"The day they found the Egg."

She nodded.

Simon was still processing the strange mass event he'd just taken part in. "Have you all done this before?"

Jace nodded. "We've seen pieces of it. But never the whole thing, and never… so intense." He blushed and looked away.

Simon grinned. *This whole scylall thing needs further exploration.* "Wait, why did everyone else have different names, but Coryn was still Coryn?"

Coryn grinned. "I changed my name to match. It was Oliver, before."

Simon laughed. He really was starting to like them.

"We've been waiting for you to complete the circuit." Jace took his hand again. "We knew there was a sixth elymm from the memories, but we didn't know who you were."

Simon closed his eyes. It was a hell of a lot to take in.

I'm not weird. Or at least, I'm the same weird as all the rest of them. He'd finally found others who matched his pattern. "What does all of this mean?" He looked up at Candace. "Why are we *here*? What do you and DARPA want from us?" Although he was pretty sure that he already knew the answer to that last one.

He'd felt the magnetic pull of the Egg, ever since he'd touched it, and it was stronger now that they'd completed the circuit. *The call of home.*

"We want to help you go back to Trillyn."

Emotions warred in his head and his heart. He was still Simon. He still had a mother here, and friends. Some friends. But to visit his homeworld… "I want to see it for myself. I think we all do." He looked around at the other travelers.

They all nodded as one.

Simon frowned as another thought occurred to him. "So, the government spent thousands—millions, probably?—to find us and bring us here, just so you could send us home?"

Candace grimaced. "Yes, but not just that. We want to establish relations with the elymm. It would likely prove... advantageous to the country. To the world. Remember the topic in class this morning?"

Simon nodded. "Fermi's Paradox."

"Very good. The world's on a roller coaster ride to oblivion, and we could use a little help. How did they break their addiction to fossil fuels, or did they never use them in the first place? Did they have to deal with climate change? Nuclear weapons? Poverty? Mass migrations?" She looked suddenly older, tired, carrying a weight he couldn't see. "Imagine what they could teach us. From what we've learned from the other travelers, the elymm are an ethical people."

"They were. That was a long time ago." Simon was still trying to process that too—more than a hundred thousand years. "What if they burned out too? Or worse... what if they've changed?"

Candace closed her eyes, the pain clearly traced in the lines at either side. "That's a fair point. It's a distinct possibility. Still, the rewards merit the risk, and they could still return on their own at any time."

"True." Simon felt the dynamic shifting between them. He was no longer her student. Instead, she was treating him as an equal. It made him feel like an adult.

"You were the ship's navigator, the pattern twister. With the Egg, we think you can build a beacon to call your people here."

Build a beacon? How am I supposed to do that? He'd never built a thing in his life that wasn't constructed of Legos.

Simon closed his eyes. He could feel the other memories. Imnyl's recollections. They were a part of him now, though they still seemed like they belonged to someone else, walled off from the things that made him *Simon*.

He fished around, tasting bits of Imnyl's thoughts, his personality. Sampling his schooling, his training to be a part of the scouting mission. *There.*

The *pattern* for the beacon.

Simon shuddered. All of his life he'd been *Strange Simon*, the odd kid who hid behind his thick glasses. Now Candace and the others wanted him to return to an alien planet. For what? To be an advocate for the human race? *Human, alien, pattern twister… It's too much.*

"I need some time." With an *I'm sorry* glance at Jace, Simon slipped off the chair and pushed his way past Candace. He headed back to the dorm, not caring if the others followed, and threw himself on the bed, staring at the wall.

The patterns in the stucco shifted, becoming a flowing river. Simon grimaced. *All the better to carry me away.* He traced the waters with his fingers, feeling the cool wetness rolling down his cheeks.

"Hey, you okay?"

Simon rolled over to find Jace standing there, staring at him. The door to the laboratory was closed behind him, and they were alone. "I don't know. How did you deal with it, when someone told you that you were a reincarnated alien?"

Jace laughed. He sat on the bed and ran his hand along Simon's neck, the strangely familiar gesture making him shudder with pleasure. "I've had longer to get used to it. I've been here since I was sixteen."

"Wow… do you ever see your family?"

"Of course. They think this is a fancy boarding school. I go home for the holidays. Sit up so I can squeeze in next to you."

Simon did as he was told, wiping his face with the back of his hand. "Don't you ever wonder why we left? Trillyn, I mean."

"Why we came here?" Jace's eyes searched his. "You don't remember?

Simon reached for Imnyl's memories. "They… kept us apart. My family and yours. Because our patterns weren't compatible?"

Jace laughed. "They were wrong about that, weren't they?" He laced his fingers with Simon's. "They said we'd bring dishonor to both our families."

The memories surfaced, becoming his own, searing their pain into his soul. Simon shuddered as more of Imnyl leaked into him. "We ran away and became scouts together."

"And now all of those doubters are all dead and turned to dust."

Simon felt a spark of pain at that too—his entire family, swallowed by the vastness of history between that moment and this one. His parents, his litter mates… "What if they were right?"

Jace leaned forward and shut him up with a kiss. The electricity between them returned, the patterns in the room shifting around them.

Jace's mind touched his.

After a second's hesitation, Simon opened himself up, letting Jace in. Letting Jlemm in. The walls between Simon and Imnyl fell, too. Pain burned bright in his mind as he fused with his former self, and then the pain became pleasure as his pattern merged with Jace/Jlemm's.

The very air sparkled as the two of them became one, floating in the breathless space between one moment and the next, flying on clouds of pleasure and connection.

Their patterns became one, and the world exploded in light. No longer were there Simon and Jace, or Imnyl and Jlemm.

Just us.

SIMON WOKE IN A DAZE, the room fuzzy around him.

The world came into focus. Next to him, Jace lay on the bed, still fully clothed.

Simon felt spent, content. That after-sex feeling where you don't want to think or move, just exist in the afterglow.

Jace turned over and looked up at him. "Hey."

Simon laughed. It was so… human. "What the hell was that?"

"*Scylall.*"

Simon shivered. "I think I could *scylall* with you all night long." All of that, without sex. *--What would it be like if we…-*

Jace grinned. "We'll find out, later." He got up and held out a hand to Simon. "Come on. We've kept the others waiting long enough."

"Okay." They were ready—it didn't need saying aloud.

They found Candace with the others still gathered around the imager, talking softly.

Candace looked up, eyebrow raised. "You okay?"

Coryn snickered, but quieted when Todd shot him a dirty look.

Simon nodded. "Jace talked me down." He felt the heat under his collar at the thought of what they'd just done, far more intimate than simple human sex. "I'll do it."

She met his gaze." Are you sure?"

He nodded. Jace came up beside him and took his hand, and that by-now familiar jolt of energy ran up his arm. "We are."

Tawny and Dorry fist bumped. "Woo hoo!"

In his ear, his phone buzzed. *-Ally, send it to voicemail.-*

-Yes, Simon.-

"What do I need to do?" He felt a growing excitement. Imnyl's memories were sharper now, as bright and recent as his own. He longed to see the Ayri racing through the sky across Dymmen Bay again, to see the beautiful lacy skyline of Amryn Tryl.

Todd cleared his throat, looking up at him. "You're the pattern twister. Just lay your hands on the Egg and twist it into what you want. Do you remember the pattern for the beacon?"

Simon closed his eyes. It shone there in the darkness, a complex pattern of reds and golds, with spikes like the tines of a fork along its back. "Yes. I can see it."

"Well, what are we waiting for?" Coryn hugged him and took his hand, dragging him unceremoniously toward the door at the back of the room. "No time like the present!"

"Coryn, be careful on the stairs. Don't break the pattern twister!" Candace sounded exasperated. "I swear, it's like herding cats with you travelers sometimes!"

The others followed, laughing and talking animatedly. Coryn led him back down the stairs, which seemed much longer this time.

The elymm practically fell over each other on the way down the stairs in their excitement.

"Slow down!" Candace shouted after them.

Simon's pattern touched Coryn's, and they flashed with laughter.

At last, they all gathered around the Egg. The six travelers made a circle, holding hands. Simon felt each of their patterns join the circuit.

As he stared at the Egg, its surface twisted and shifted like mercury.

Simon waited for the flash like last time, the blow that would knock him back against the wall, but nothing happened. He glanced at Jace, doubtfully. "Should I…?"

Jace brushed his fingers along Simon's neck, eliciting a shiver. *Yes, Simon. Do it.*

Simon reached for the Egg.

His phone buzzed again in his ear. Frowning, he let go of Cory's and Jace's hands. "Ally, what's the message?"

-It's a text from your mother: "Hey Simon, you okay? I love you." Would you like to reply?-

Simon stared at the Egg.

In all the excitement, he'd almost forgotten about her—his mother, the woman who had raised him, who had dragged her son from doctor to doctor to find out what was wrong with him. Who had all but given up her own life for him for eighteen years.

How will I tell her? He looked up at the other travelers gathered around him. *-Not right now.-*

-Understood.-

"What is it?" Todd cocked his head, staring at him from under his blue baseball cap.

In response, Simon took Coryn's hand again on the right, and Jace's on the left.

Coryn nodded, and they took Todd's hand. Soon all of them connected again as their patterns sought their joining points with one another.

The bond came more naturally this time, their patterns merging like old friends recently reunited.

Simon closed his eyes and thought of his mother, sharing his memories with the other travelers.

That trip to the doctor as a kid, and many more besides. Her making him breakfast in bed for his birthday. Doing his math homework with him on a school night. Hugging him tight when he'd graduated high school with top honors, face beaming with pride. Holding him when he came home, crying after the kids called him *Strange Simon.*

He'd been about to leave all that behind for this new family who he didn't know—not really.

Were any of them the same as they had been that fateful day a hundred thousand years before?

I don't want to leave. This is my home now.

More images filled the circuit. Coryn with their older brother Max. Jace and his father, fishing on a lake in the summertime. Dorry and Tawny at Thanksgiving with their extended family at Lake Tahoe. Still more flooded the link, feelings and memories and faces and a sensation of warmth akin to what he'd first felt when the six of them had connected.

"Am I crazy?" Simon said it aloud for Candace's benefit. He opened his eyes to find them all staring at him. "This feels like fate, right? I mean, I'm not human." He frowned. "But I'm not exactly elymm, either."

Candace frowned, looking at each of them. "You all having cold feet?"

Todd nodded. "We don't want to go. Not for good." Todd spoke for them all. "All of us were born *here*—Earth is our home. We're not aliens. Not anymore."

A mental flicker of dissent from Jace. "Don't you guys want to know? Who we were? Where we came from?"

Simon felt the same ache from himself and through the circuit.

A silence descended on the room. It was an impossible choice.

Simon stared at his feet, unsure what to do.

"Why not do both?" Coryn's voice echoed through the silent chamber, and they blushed. "I mean, why not call them *and* stay here? Or visit Trillyn and then come back?"

Simon stared at him. "Can we… can we do that?"

Candace frowned, her eyes skittering back and forth between them as she thought over his question. A smile spread across her face and her eyes brightened. "Why not? We're going to need ambassadors, after all."

Jace squeezed his hand, and *warmth and love* came through the link.

Simon gauged their assent. They all nodded in unison. "That would work." He grinned. They were like the Borg, but he didn't care. *Our own little Borg family.* "Ally, send a text to my mom: "*I'm okay. I have big news—I'll tell you more soon. Love you.*" Send."

-Sent.-

"So… should I?" Simon looked around and felt the assent from his new family.

Jace met his gaze, his eyes twinkling. *-Yes, do it.-*

Simon reached for the Egg.

About Paraidolia

Another story inspired by a word. This one was in an Italian story we read in our study group—strangely, it's exactly the same spelling in both English and Italian.

I was intrigued by the idea of seeing faces and recognizable objects in random patterns and data. What if, in addition to being able to see order in chaos, my hero could also create it? And so the story was born.

THE SYSTEM

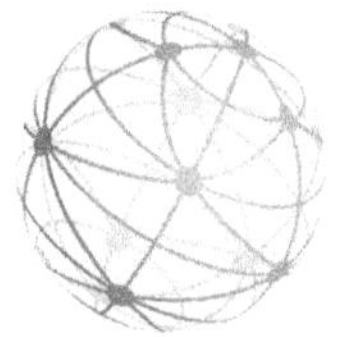

Dammit.

Hank stared at his three-dee screen in disbelief.

"We're sorry. We are unable to renew 'My Gay Cyborg Boyfriend.' This book has been checked out by the System."

What the hell was the System doing reading gay porn? He'd been crazy-busy, called in three times that week for unpaid overtime in Reprogramming. People were losing their shit in record numbers these days.

He blamed the System.

"The System will save mankind," they'd said when they launched it two years before. "It will reorganize every aspect of our society." He'd even helped create the monster. Hell, it was a paycheck.

Bad idea, though. Fucking recipe for a Terminator, if you asked him. Not that they had.

The reality had turned out to be much more banal. All those new "sharing economy" jobs? Now run by the system. And people had little to do from day to day, as The System took over more and more of their daily work. *Thank god for Government Cheese.* He snorted.

Autos that flew themselves. Hotel rooms that self-cleaned and rented themselves. Hell, he bet even movies would watch themselves one of these days.

And now the *goddamned* system was reading his library book.

He'd had enough.

He pulled out his touchboard and accessed the grid, logging in with a dummy account he'd created years before. For all its complexity, programming hardware was still a lot more straightforward than the wetware of people's brains.

When he'd helped build the System, he'd left himself a backdoor, just in case. He'd been an untrusting bastard even then.

Was it still there?

Yes!

He snuck inside. This was gonna take some time, as the System was spread throughout Thundercloud. He'd have to lock the door behind him.

He grinned.

Time to give the System a little renewal.

About The System

Every year we ask hundreds of writers to put together a 300 word story based on a one-word theme, for the annual Queer Sci Fi Flash Fiction Contest. In 2017, we took a little of our own medicine, writing some sample stories for the QSF site. 'The System' was mine.

LAMPLIGHTER

Panting heavily, back against a whitewashed wall, Fen prayed for the shaking to end. He mumbled one of the Guild Cantos:

We are keepers of light
In the river of night
when the black tides of darkness advance.

Then he ran as if Davien the Betrayer were after him. Behind him, walls that had stood since long before he was born crashed to dust, and the smell of char and the metallic tang of blood hung heavily in the morning air. Clouds of smoke and dust blotted out the spindle above, blocking its golden light, and Disembodied voices screamed around him. He needed something to light the way….

Fen Theora'son woke with a start, sweat-drenched, alone. He looked around—his narrow bedroom was empty, with only the whispering of the wind through the open window. He ran his fingers through his black, sweat-drenched hair, unsettled. *Just a dream.*

Why not believe in the world-mind too, while I'm at it? Fen snorted. His mother had spun tales of the creature that made the winds blow and the light of the spindle shine and the rain fall inside this pebble of a world, but he'd always taken it for a fairy tale.

Another of her old stories sparked in his head. The one about liminals, who in his mother's telling were half human and half something else, people who did magical things, like talking mind to mind or communing with the world by touch. Who dreamed strange dreams that often came true.

I'm letting the quiet and the darkness get to me. He laid back and closed his eyes, pulling his blanket up over his lanky form, but the easy rhythms of sleep were lost to him. The hard straw pallet that was the journeyman lamplighter's only bed for his first year was worn down and flat, but at least he had a bed frame now. And his own small room.

There'd been no new straw for weeks to stuff the mattress with. The scent of Lewin's amber skin was gone too, worn out of the sheets like an old half-forgotten song. Anger creased red at the edges of his mind, but he thrust it away. *I won't let him do this to me.* Slowly it receded.

Sleep eluded him, dream fragments and unwelcome memories and overheard rumors chasing one another in his head like a pack of street dogs. So many rumors, filling the city like worms in a rotten apple.

As the earth shook and the Enders—a wool-headed pack of idiots who claimed knowledge from the world-mind—proclaimed the apocalypse, his own world had shrunk down to almost nothing. Buffoons like Luz Tamars'son, Fen's cousin, who'd follow a sheep to slaughter without thought.

Would the gates still be closed when the spindle lit up the inside of Forever with its golden morning light? The council sat behind closed doors, seeing no one, only sending out pages. Outside Thyre's walls, food was rotting in the fields as farmers were locked out.

Fen's stomach grumbled. Perhaps his vivid dreams were the sign of an upset stomach, fed too little from stores that were stale and old.

Dreams of a morning with no light, of falling walls and unearthly screams. And a room so full of light it hurt his eyes.

Would there be war? It was a word unused since the Chaos Years.

I just want to sleep.

He closed his eyes and drifted off into a troubled rest.

FEN BLEW out the little candle on the windowsill and looked out at the city. The walls of the world curved up and around to meet over his head, extending north and south like a giant version of the pipes which carried water throughout the buildings of the guild.

The outer walls of the city followed the arc of the world to meet somewhere overhead, forming two tall rings with the quarters of the city carving out smaller rings of their own inside. High above Fen's head, the place where they med was hidden by the faint silver night light of the spindle that ran above him from one horizon to the other.

As he watched, the spindle flared into glorious life, a golden wave of morning illumination riding it past Thyre and on toward Darlith and Micavery, brightening the inside of world.

Morning light crossed Thyre in little steps too as pollen began to glow and the few plants shone with their own morning light. The very air around him shimmered. Night gave way to the golden glow of daylight that leapt over the far wall of the city and crossed into the plains and forests beyond, the trees and grasses beginning to glow.

Guild apprentices were out already, extinguishing the lamps on each street. Lights from windows set in high, white-washed walls blinked out one by one, as did the occasional light on the back of a wagon that passed by below.

Fen pulled on his tunic and breeches and washed his face in the mallowwood basin in one corner of the tiny room. He sat at his tiny wooden desk, where long sheets of parchment, curled at the ends, held the month's ledgers for Master Harmon's accounts. He'd spent hours the evening before calculating the dues owed by the various city merchants to the guild account.

Everyone wanted light at night to fend off the fear in the air, so the numbers were inordinately high, but the prospects of collecting it seemed dubious with counselors and commoners alike shuttered behind locked doors. But that was an apprentice's problem, not a journeyman's. *Why do we even bother to light so many empty streets?*

The need for light is reason enough. The guild maxim came without thought.

Why did I ever want to be a lamplighter? The seven guilds of Thyre were the main source of coin for Thyrian youth. Unless someone's family was wealthy, or their parents were shopkeepers or farmers, one ended up in a guild or the guard.

Fen sighed. He dipped pen to ink and got to work.

A while later, a knock at the door startled him. He was glad he'd set the pen down, or he'd have ruined one of the ledger pages. Master Harmon would skin him alive for the loss, journeyman or no. "Who is it?" Annoyance colored his tone.

The door swung open.

"Alissa…" Half-exasperated, his lips quirked in amusement. She didn't respect personal boundaries very well, but he'd gotten used to it.

"At least I knocked, this time." The apprentice grinned, ignoring his annoyance. Like many in the guild, Alissa said she'd been drawn to service by a need to belong to *something* in these strange times. Why would someone whose father was a city councilor *need* to do anything? She'd never said, and he'd never asked. His own father was a master leatherworker who'd raised his family on a minor landholder's farm outside the city walls. Fen hadn't talked to them for years.

"Up carousing with the boys?" Alissa grinned.

"Not last night," His own smile felt pained.

"Too bad. Might have done your sour mood some good."

"As if *you'd* know." His wasn't the only lonely bed. There were few secrets in the packed dormitory of the Guild House. "You didn't come here just to tease me."

She shook her head. "Not *just* for that. Master Harmon sent me to check on your accounting. He's got a task for us to perform, if you're done. A *great privilege*." She eyed his untidy stack of papers.

"I'm done, for now." He shuffled them into some semblance of organization. No lowly apprentice was going to call him on the carpet. Especially not *this one*. "What did Harmon want?"

She grinned, a look of pure mischief, and he knew he was in trouble. "Better bring your wetboots."

As Fen sloshed through sewer water up to his knees, he tried to concentrate on the *great privilege* he'd been given. The sewer tunnel was filled with the terrible stench of human waste—he was thankful their small lamps didn't cast too much light. Beneath the streets of Thyre, the Underground was a maze of tunnels and sewer lines that even the most experienced journeyman knew little about. Few outside the Sanitation Guild did, and he was happy to leave it to them.

This was his first time in the realm that few in the city even knew existed. The Lamplighter's Guild kept barrels of luthiel down here in locked storerooms. Who knew how much there was, and what else was hidden down here?

"You get used to the smell, eventually, they tell me." At least he hadn't been able to see any of the things in the water that brushed against his wet boots, the soles of which squished for the first couple steps out of the water.

"Pay attention to the map, journeyboy. I don't want to get lost." Alissa's eyes were wide as she looked at the dark walls.

Fen shivered at the thought. If you were still here when your light ran out, you might never find your way back to the surface.

They came to the last crossing on the hastily scribbled map. Water flowed along the right-hand tunnel while the left-hand one sloped up in relative dryness. They left the underground river behind, climbing up the passageway until it dead-ended in a flat white wall. Or at least he supposed it must have been white at one time; now it was covered with a thin layer of moss or algae, which gave off a faint greenish glow outside the lanterns' pale light.

"This is the place." He scraped away the muck along the right side of the wall to reveal a recess with a series of metal handles. He pulled them up and down in the sequence Master Harmon had given him.

Nothing happened.

With a sigh, he reset them and tried again. Still nothing.

"Let me try."

With a sigh, he handed Alissa the paper. She flicked the levers, and this time, the wall slid aside with a loud grinding protest.

Fen frowned.

"That one was a six, not an eight. Master Harmon has sloppy handwriting."

Fen snorted. "I'll tell him you think so." He squeezed through the doorway, concerned that it might slam shut on him, and found himself in a room filled with hundreds of sealed wooden barrels. He whistled… so much luthiel. One barrel would light half the streetlamps in the city—this room represented a stockpile almost beyond imagining.

Why had Master Harmon sent him for this? Fen was still a journeyman. If he wanted, he could steal them and put a large dent in the guild's monopoly, if not ruin it altogether. He wouldn't, but why would Harmon take that chance?

Alissa stared at the vast store of barrels. "Why us?"

"I don't know, 'Liss."

"I didn't know the guild even had this much luthiel." She shook her head. "Father would be apoplectic."

Fen managed a smile. "Their claim of a limited supply would fall apart—they'd have to lower prices." How many other storerooms like this were there? *Too many secrets.*

Alissa's expression hardened. "The guild should light the streets for free at a time like this."

You're not wrong. He was a journeyman, though. Such decisions were above his paygrade. "Come on. Let's get what we came for and get out of here." Time enough to think things over later.

She nodded, but she wasn't satisfied. They'd known each other too long—it was gnawing at her.

Between them, they lifted one of the heavy barrels, turning it on its side, and rolled it out of the vault. He closed the door behind them, and they set off for the surface. "You can't tell anyone about this."

Alissa bit her lip. "Father should know."

He stopped the barrel and held up his lantern to look her in the eye. "You took an oath to the guild. You could get both of us kicked out. Promise me you won't say anything, at least until we have a chance to think this over."

"It's not right—"

"I know. Promise?"

At last she nodded. "Promise."

"Good. Come on, let's get this to the surface. I want to wash off the stench of this place before it becomes permanent."

Something to light the way.

A loud thump outside Fen's door disturbed his sleep, bringing him out of his recurring dream. He brushed it aside, looking around blearily.

His bed was empty, and he felt cold and alone. *I need to see Lewin.*

He got up and pulled on his clothes. He scribbled out a hasty note on one of the precious sheets of parchment he'd saved from his accounting work and folded it neatly, sealing it with a dab of melted wax. Then he crept to the door. It opened softly for once, the wood drier than the desert sand. Even the weather had been odd lately.

Fen slipped out of his room and down the hall, past the other journeymen dorms. All the doors were closed, and only Caswin's had light glimmering under the crack. At the end of the hall, he eased the outer door open just far enough to squeeze out into the central courtyard.

The white fountain at its heart, with its stature of Andrissa Hammond holding aloft a luthiel lantern, trickled quietly in the night. Everything was serene, quiet, normal.

Softly he closed the door behind him and made his way along

the inner wall around the courtyard, quiet as a cat. The fountain's flickering lamplight cast slivers of gold light across the open space.

Fen reached the gate that led out into the city, hoping it would be unguarded. When Ersa was on duty, she often slept through the middle part of her shift.

No such luck. He was met at the gate by Archer Tamars'son, who poked his head out of the guard's kiosk at his approach. "Bit late for a stroll, isn't it?" It was well past guild curfew, for journeymen and apprentices alike.

"Sorry, Arch, but I *have* to go out."

"You know the rules, Fen…."

"And I *have* to break them, Arch. It's important...come on, I'll be back well before light."

Archer stared at him. The man had come with Fen and Kerrith on several hunts into the steppe. They respected each other, and Fen had a good reputation in the guild.

"Please, Archer."

The guard sighed and opened the gate. "Go. Be back before shift change. It'll be on *my* head if you're late."

Fen nodded. "Thanks, Arch, I owe you." He slipped out into the cobblestoned city streets. It was quiet, everyone in the city waiting for *something*. Echoes of his dreams haunted him. The shakes had diminished to an occasional background noise, a rumble or groan issuing from the ground beneath his feet. *Not much of an improvement.*

He crossed through the rings that defined the districts of Thyre, making his way from the guild quarters near the desert wall through the normally bustling lower rings. Even there he found silence—a few taverns were open, but most of the patrons looked more lost than drunk. Still, he'd left his pouch behind; this was not a place to wander at night with a sack full of coin.

His fever-dreams had convinced him—he had to talk to Lewin.

If things were over between them, let them be over, but he had to know for sure.

At last he reached the alleyway behind the Masons' Guildhouse. Sure no one was watching, Fen slipped into the narrow alley between buildings. The walls were uncomfortably close, and he imagined them crashing down to crush him. He pushed the disturbing image out of his head.

Softly glowing vines grew thickly here, vines that the Lamplighter's Guild would have seen torn down long ago had they not belonged to another guild. Each guild was sovereign, and occasionally they thumbed their noses at one another. Fen snorted. *Like overgrown children.*

Handy for him though. Finding the right spot, he placed the letter between his teeth and took hold of one of the thick ropes, levering himself up the wall.

He froze as noises spilled from an open window above. Someone was violating curfew, in the most carnal way possible. Fen grinned.

The sounds continued unabated, and after a moment, so did he.

Lewin's room was on the second floor, a journeyman's like his. There was no light coming from the window, but the shutters were open. Taking a deep breath, Fen let go of the vine with one hand to swing around the gaping shutters to grasp the windowsill. A flick of his wrist, and the sealed letter sailed into the room.

He didn't wait to see where it landed. With haste, he scurried down the wall, making more noise than he had on the way up. His hand slipped, and he fell the remaining few feet, scraping his hands on the way down and landing on the cobblestone alley hard enough to knock the breath out of him.

He gasped softly until the air returned to his lungs, then wiped the blood on his breeches, cursing the likely stain it would leave. He had no time to waste, and it wasn't safe to linger there. He scrambled down the alley, disappearing into the darkness of the street just as someone popped their head out of a lighted window above.

Back in his own bed, dreams swarmed through his head—images of dark, wet passageways that twisted like snakes beneath the city, full of glowing venom. Fen was lost in their darkness, calling out Lewin's name...

Something awakened him again, bringing him out of yet another apocalyptic dream where the ground shook itself into powder and a woman's screams filled the air. He sat up in the pale light of the spindle's night glow and glanced around the room, looking for the source of the noise that had brought him out of his slumber. It had to be near daylight.

He pulled himself up with a hand on his mattress and winced—his hands were sore from the fall.

A pebble clattered across the floor near the window, skittering to rest beside his cot. *Lewin.*

He nearly leapt out of bed, scrambling toward the window. But just short of that gaping portal, he stopped. He ran a hurried hand through his hair, wincing again. *He came. That has to mean something.* He took a deep breath, and then looked out onto the street below. "Lewin?"

Lewin grinned, his teeth white even in the darkness. "Let me up, Fen."

Like *Rapunzel.* Fen pulled a knotted rope from beneath the mattress, playing it out down the wall.

Lewin was athletic and had used the rope countless times before. Soon he was climbing through the window into the room to give Fen a bear hug. "You took quite a chance, coming up to my room tonight." Lewin's voice was low as he searched Fen's face. "Someone else might have that room by now, and might have read your...sentiments."

Fen blushed. "I'm sorry. I just needed to talk." He sank down onto his mattress, back against the wall. "It's been so long...." He leaned over to light one of the smaller luthiel candles on the floor beside the bed. It cast a golden, flickering light across the room.

It was Lewin's turn to blush. He sat down on the bed heavily next to Fen. "Yes, it has. I've meant to come. To *talk*."

Fen was keenly aware of the small distance between them, of the shape of Lewin's unshaven jaw, of his scent. He wanted to reach out, to touch that face. Instead, he kept his hands resolutely at his side. "You're here now."

Lewin nodded. "Your letter...well, I had to come. This hasn't been easy for me either." He reached up to stroke Fen's cheek gently with the back of his hand, and Fen shivered.

"Is it over between us?" *Don't let yourself feel anything.*

Lewin pulled his hand back as if he'd been stung. He stood and moved to the darkened window to stare silently out at the city.

Fen's internal alarm blared at him. *Something's wrong.*

Lewin's head dropped, and his voice was so low, Fen almost didn't hear it. "There's a woman, Fen. I know—I don't want it, but she's a good match. My family wants me to—"

Fen went stand next to Lewin. He stared out the window at the darkness beyond. It was still dark out. Something was very wrong.

Lewin looked at him, eyes narrowed. "Fen, I'm so sorry—"

Fen shook his head in annoyance, barely hearing the words. "Not now, Lew. Listen."

As if in response, the Dawn Tower pealed out its *first light* chimes. They sounded ominous in the unnatural darkness. The sense of wrong vibrated inside him like a plucked string.

"Lew, where's the morning glow?" Panic rose in his gut, but he shoved it down again. "It's first light—why is it still dark outside?"

Above, the spindle's silver night-glow was fading, leaving the city in near-total darkness. Lewin stared at him, lit only by the lone candle in the tiny room.

That's when the wailing began. Disembodied voices screaming and crying out in the darkness outside his window. *It's my dream.* Fen cursed himself for being right. *But how?*

"What in the blazes?" Lewin stared at him.

The door flew open.

Fen gaped, realizing Lewin was still in his room. Like that really mattered right now.

Luckily it was only Alissa. She gave Lewin a cursory glance before blurting out her news. "Fen, the masters are sending everyone out to light all the lamps. There's no daylight!"

Fen nodded. "Lewin is—"

Alissa's smile was grim. "Doesn't matter. Bring him. We can use every hand we've got."

FEN REFILLED the lantern with luthiel, enough golden liquid filling the small basin to last for at least a day. The golden substance glowed on its own, like the trees and shrubs of the world.

The rumors were flying fast and thick. It was the end of the world. Or the mythical world-mind had re-awoken and was seeking its revenge. Or Davien the Betrayer had returned to rule them all.

Fen didn't know what to believe, so he stuck to his job. He checked the lamp's mantle—it was still in good condition, but if they had to burn the lanterns night and day, they would deteriorate twice as fast. Satisfied, he sparked the lamp, and a comforting golden glow lit up the world around him. It gave off light but no heat.

From his high perch, he looked down the long, winding Merchant's Way—they had a long distance to go yet before they were done for the morning. *More like perpetual night.* He shoved that unhelpful thought aside.

The guild had instructed them to light every other lamp, claiming a shortage of luthiel. People needed light, especially right now when darkness threatened to consume them all. *Greedy bastards.* There was more than enough luthiel hidden away in the sewers.

Along Tassian Way, the next street over, another team was lighting lamps too, a scene repeated across the city. Even the apprentices like Alissa had been pressed into lighting service for the first time. In the distance there was a deep rumbling sound. The shakes were coming more constantly now.

Fen clambered down the pole, his feet finding the stepping bars by instinct. Lew met him at the bottom and filled his pouch with luthiel for the next lamp. "Thanks, Lew."

Across the street, another one lit up, and Alissa waved at them as she descended. "This is a lot of work."

Lewin laughed. "You're telling me."

Fen gave him the side-eye. "You're just carrying the supplies. Try going up and down a lamp pole a few hundred times!"

Lewin laughed, and so did Fen, a welcome release in the tense dark morning.

There were few passers-by in the darkness—most people were staying inside, frightened of the darkness.

They proceeded down the lane, taking turns with the lamps, all the way to the Open Market. The one place that had never needed, nor wanted, the lamplighter's guild's lights before today. The Open Market was a wide plaza in the center of the lowest ring of the city. Merchants from the cities around Forever came here to hawk their wares, and there was always abundant light from the sky above to illuminate their dealings with one another. But not this morning.

The market was desolate today, empty of the colors and smells that usually pervaded it. The vendors had vanished, one by one, over the last few days, and now the space was vast, empty and dark. That, more than anything, rattled Fen.

Alissa looked across the plaza. "Dismal, isn't it? Father says the merchants are afraid to come to market now. No one's buying, and there have been too many thefts."

Fen nodded. There was a darkness in his soul that seemed well-matched to the darkness outside. It was getting colder too, a bitter chill he'd never felt before that worked its way up from his fingers and into his wrists. Fen's ears were frozen too, and his nose was running. He could see his breath in the golden lamp light. They stared at each other in surprise.

"It really is the end of the world." Lewin's own breath made a small cloud of fog.

"Come on. I want to *feel* the darkness." Fen stepped into the marketplace, not waiting for his friends to follow.

After a moment, Alissa and Lewin did. Neither brought a light.

The last streetlamp diminished behind them, becoming only a star's pinprick of light to the darkness. The cobblestone rocks of the plaza were worn smooth by the passage of many feet, cartwheels and horses over the years, but the near-invisible ground felt solid, safe under his feet. The darkness here felt somehow less threatening than the shadows that clung to the streets and alleyways.

At last they reached the center of the plaza, where the pinpricks of light from the lamps of the surrounding streets were equally distant. Fen stopped to stare up at the black night sky.

The spindle was always there, a constant thread of light night or day, as sure as life and breath. Now it had vanished, and his world was cast adrift.

Lewin and Alissa came up beside him, vague shadows, each putting a hand on his shoulder.

"What happens next?" Alissa's voice seemed small in the vast dark space.

"I don't know." He felt better having them there with him in the darkness.

"Look!" Fen felt Lewin's arm shift upward.

"What?" He stared at the inky sky.

"It's *still there*. Faint as hell, but still there."

Fen searched the sky. At last, he saw it—a whisper-thin hairline of silver light. He reached up as if he could touch it, and the darkness inside him melted. "There's hope."

In the darkness, Lewin's hand slid into his, squeezing it tightly.

Light the way.

The city needed light. The guild had barrels and barrels of luthiel stored in the sewers.

Fen frowned. He was bad enough with directions aboveground, let alone in the labyrinthine passages below the city, and Master Harmon had taken back the directions he'd provided for their underground expedition.

The world shook again, so hard that it knocked them to the ground. Fen caught himself, his abraded palms slamming into the hard stone. *Fuck.* As he caught himself on the smooth stones, a tingling ran through him.

The world changed and shifted, and he could *feel* the stones beneath him, not just the ones he was touching, but the whole of the market, each connected to the next in a long chain of slow-moving *life*. And beneath that, the tangled tunnels of the sewers.

Fen. The voice was weak, thready, but determined.

Fen sat up and looked around. "Alissa? Lewin?"

There was no answer.

He stood, and his eyes began to adjust to the darkness. He was in a long valley, the wind whispering through the grass at his feet. He looked up and the sky was full of tiny lanterns.

Stars. His mind supplied the word. He stared at them in wonder—something no one living inside Forever had ever seen.

Fen. The voice filled the air, filled his head, stronger this time.

He turned to find a tall stone tower looming over him, blotting out the sky. "Who are you?"

The world-mind. You can call me Elle. She sounded tired. World weary.

The world-mind was a myth as strange as the stars. Fen looked around for the source of the voice, wondering if he was losing his mind. "What do you want?"

I'm dying, Fen.

The stars above began to wink out of existence, one by one.

Fen frowned. It couldn't be true. He *must* be dreaming again. And yet, he felt the weight of it. The passing of something vast and almost unimaginable from the world. "What can I do?"

Light the way for them, Fen. Get them through the night. The voice was fainter now, as if it came from much farther away.

"Is this the end of the world?"

It is an ending. *But it's a beginning too. Have hope, Fen Theora'son. You know what to do.* Then it was gone, and the strange starlit valley was too, leaving Fen alone in the darkness of the market.

"You okay, Fen?" Lewin's hand was warm on Fen's face, his outline barely visible above him.

"Yeah, just hit my head." They'd never believe him if he told them the truth. The world-mind was real, and she had spoken to *him*. How was that even possible?

Still, Elle was right. There was more to do this night than

lighting lamps and cowering behind the walls of the guild. "I know what to do."

He explained what he needed and could almost see the shocked looks on Alissa and Lewin's faces.

"How will we find our way back there?" Alissa sounded uncertain, but somehow firmer. "This could get us thrown out of the guild."

"You just have to trust me. Do you trust me?" He was as sure about this as he'd ever been about anything. Whatever the consequences.

Lewin squeezed his hand. "I'm in. Sometimes you have to take a chance."

Do you mean…? Fen had to let that go, for now. "So we're agreed?"

"Damn it all to hell." Fen could hear Alissa grinding her teeth. "I'm in too."

"Come on then." Fen didn't want to lose his newfound courage. "We have a lot to do."

THE WALLS of the sewer shook around them, the water sloshing up their sides like waves on the sea. Fen stopped to touch the rock, and the strange *sense of place* flooded through him again. It was like touching the nerves of the world; as if he were, however momentarily, a small part of them. It was a strange thought.

He was tired, but he pushed himself onward. They were almost there. He hoped Lewin had managed to round up the other things they needed above ground.

"A few more like that and there won't be any more us." Fen looked around grimly. Ahead, the passageway connected with a cross-shaft. "Almost there."

Alissa nodded. "This looks familiar." She looked as tired as he felt.

During one of the more recent shakes, there had been a distant crash behind them, followed by a rush of water through the passage, bringing the level well up their chests for a moment. Fool chance they were taking, but what else could they do?

The glow of the moss on the walls was stronger here. Strange that the moss was alight while the rest of the world above was dark. Better to think on that than to imagine what was in the muck that sucked at his boot soles with every step. They were filthy enough with the sewer water as it was. He imagined not even his own mother would let him in the door after this, not before he had a long, hot bath.

Alissa followed his thoughts. "Bit of a mess, aren't we? I haven't had this much fun since we played salamander in the rain outside the walls as kids. Remember?"

He laughed, some of the tension broken. "We never smelled this bad." He looked up to see the tunnel branch. "Left here."

Wearily they climbed the slope to the hidden room, where he stared blankly at the opening mechanism. *What was the blazing sequence?* The dying world-mind couldn't help him with that one.

"Let me." Alissa slipped past him and moved the levers, and the door slid noisily open.

"How did you do that?"

She snorted. "I paid attention."

Fen laughed. "Ten barrels should be enough. Come on, let's get them moving."

They took turns putting the barrels on their sides and rolling them down the slope to rest just above the fork in the tunnel.

Alissa was right—they'd be thrown out of the guild for this. They were stealing precious guild property. Fen no longer cared. It was a small enough offense at the end of the world, when everyone needed light and hope.

When they had all the barrels lined up, they tied a rope around one of the small metal loops on each side of the first one and eased it into the water, holding it steady.

Alissa wrestled the second one next to the first, and they tied the two together. In short order, they had all ten in a long floating convoy. "Ready?"

Alissa grabbed the lantern and rejoined him in the fetid water. "Ready as I'll ever be." They started off, hauling the barrels upstream along the slow-moving waters of the sewer. They maneuvered the casks of luthiel carefully around a corner, with Fen checking the way every ten paces.

"Let's hope your boyfriend comes through for us."

Fen stared at her. "He's not… Lewin's not my boyfriend." Cross-guild relationships between journeymen were strictly forbidden.

Alissa snorted. "So our dear mason journeyman was in your bedroom before first light this morning to *inspect the walls*?"

Fen sighed. Alissa was no idiot. "He—we were together. Once. But now—"

The world shook violently, and Alissa fell, grabbing at one of the barrels. It slipped from her grasp and she splashed into the water. The lantern light went out, plunging them into pitch-black darkness.

"'Liss! You okay back there?" Fen peered into the darkness from the front of their little caravan of barrels.

Someone spat and cursed. "I think so." Fen heard water dripping. "Sweet Ariadne that's foul." She spat out something—Fen didn't want to know. "It's gonna take a week for me to get the stench out. But how are we going to get out of here now?" Her voice was edged with panic.

"Stay calm." He reached out to find the wall. "Ouch."

"You okay?"

He nodded, then realized she couldn't see him. "Yeah. The rock's rough, is all." His palms were still sore from the fall down Lewin's wall.

He put his palm against the stone, and awareness flooded through him once again. "I can get us home."

Half an hour later, they reached the sewer entrance, cheered by the glow of the luthiel lantern they'd left hanging on the landing. One by one, they untied the barrels and hauled them up out of the water to sit up on dry ground.

I did it. Fen stared back along the pitch-black tunnel in wonder. He'd heard of people like him—liminals, they'd been called—who could speak to the world-mind. It was a strange legend out of the depths of time. *Apparently more than legend. No time to figure it out now.*

Together, they carried the first barrel up the stone stairs and out the once-locked gate onto the city street, where they were greeted by an unexpected multitude.

"You made it!" Lewin hugged him, then backed away, his nose wrinkling in disgust. "And you brought the stench with you."

Fen grimaced. "Not much choice. We were in the sewers, after all." He looked at the assembled crowd under the golden light of the streetlamps. "You brought some friends."

Lewin nodded. "Every one of the journeymen and apprentices I could find from the Mason's Guild. And some of *their* friends too."

Fen looked around at the crowd. They were all his age, give or take. He even recognized a few faces from his own guild—Caswin and Jacob and Tyler.

Cas grinned. "If they kick you out of the guild, they'll have to kick all of us out. It's about time we changed things around here."

There was a general cheer of agreement.

Lewin turned to address the crowd. "There's more barrels down there. We need a few strong bodies to bring them up."

As some of the others streamed past him and into the stairwell that led down to the sewer, Fen whistled in appreciation. "How did you do this?"

Lewin grinned. We're all tired of the guilds, Fen. Things need to change. If we survive the long night, they *will* change."

It was Fen's turn to grin.

"But how are we going to distribute all this luthiel?"

Lewin turned to Alissa and laughed. "You look like a half-drowned rat who took a dip in Shit River."

Alissa grumbled. "Close enough."

"That's a good question." If they could secure a wagon somewhere, they could deliver it from house to house. But that would take forever.

A creaking sound caught Fen's attention.

"Ah, the Potter's Guild is here." Lewin gestured to an arriving wagon loaded with baskets, like an answer to Fen's prayers. "Dera Thessas'daughter's a journeyman in the Potter's Guild."

A woman with silver hair set down the reins and jumped down to greet them. She held out her hand to Lewin. "I'm Dera. You must be Lewin? Del said you were a handsome bastard. Quite a movement you've started here."

"Fen here did it. I just rounded up the troops."

Dera turned to appraise him. "This little thing? Nice to meet you, Fen the revolutionary."

Fan laughed in spite of himself. "Hardly. I just had an idea."

She grinned. "Every good revolution starts with one."

Fen looked over at her wagon. "What did you bring us?"

Dera led them to the back and opened one of the baskets. Inside were bunches of ceramic stoppered vases of all colors, nestled in homecloth.

This was going to work. "I'd hug you, but—"

Desa's laugh was deep and hearty. "Keep your distance, sewer boy. You can thank me later."

Fen's mind was racing. He was born to organize things like this. "We need teams. We have ten barrels—we'll also need dippers, and runners to distribute the luthiel—"

"What in Saint Ana's name is going on here?" The roar silenced all activity.

Fen looked up to see Master Harmon descending upon him, dressed in his nightclothes, his long gray hair waving around his head like a horde of snakes. He took Lewin's hand.

The Guild Master stopped half a meter away and glared at him, and then Lewin, and finally at the barrels and baskets.

"It's—I can explain. Everyone needs light—"

Harmon's gesture cut him off. "I don't want to hear it. You *do* know this is a dismissible offense?"

The other journeymen gathered around them in a circle, their gazes hardening.

Harmon looked around at each of them. The Lamplighters' Guild members blanched but stood their ground.

Harmon muttered under his voice.

Fen stared at him, waiting for the word. Waiting to hear he'd been let go, that he'd be out on the street come first light. If first light ever came again.

Harmon opened his mouth.

Alissa threw herself between them. "It's not Fen's fault. It was all my idea. Dismiss me…sir."

"'Liss, no—"

Harmon looked at him, then Alissa, and then back at him

again. "I *ought* to dismiss the lot of you. And not just from the Lamplighter's Guild—I could report each of you to your own respective guilds." He looked around the circle. "But sometimes you need to be young to see what has to be done." He eased Alissa aside and begrudgingly put a hand on Fen's shoulder. "You're right, Mr. Theora'son. We need to *light the way.*"

There was a collective sigh of disbelief from the journeymen.

Fen stared at him. Those words—it couldn't be a coincidence. "Yes, sir."

"What can I do to help, son?" A sly grin played across his face but was gone in an instant.

He wanted *me to do this*, Fen thought furiously. He needed a revolutionary movement bigger than one man for change to happen. "We could use some barrel taps, sir. And more runners."

Harmon nodded. "Consider it done. Caswin, Tyler, to me."

As the journeymen organized themselves into work teams, Fen turned to Lewin and Alissa. "Spin be damned, I think we did it."

Alissa laughed. "Not yet. But with the Guild Master's help…"

Fen turned to Lewin. "Lew… things are changing. I don't want to face it all alone. If we survive this long night…."

Lewin took his hand, pulled him in for a kiss. It was long and sweet, and when it was over, Lewin laid his hands on Fen's face and looked in his eyes. "Like I said, sometimes you have to take a chance."

FEN LED Lewin down the hall to his room. No more subterfuge. No more hiding.

It had been an arduously long night, and no one knew if daylight would ever come again. If the spindle would ever flare to life. If there was a world-mind, would it ever wake up? It was also bitterly cold. If this was the end, Fen was determined to spend it with Lewin.

The shaking had subsided a few hours before. Fen didn't know if that portended good, or ill.

They reached his room and Fen led Lewin to the open window. He wrapped his blanket around the two of them for warmth, and together they looked out at the lights that burned in every window of the city—golden pinpricks of light that lit Thyre like the fabled stars inside the world-mind.

"The end of the world is more beautiful than I ever imagined."

Fen grinned. "I'd give it all up, just for this moment." Somehow it had all worked out. They'd brought a little hope to the world and he still had his post. For all the good that would do.

"Fen, look!"

Once again he followed Lewin's voice.

The spindle was slowly flaring to life, a golden glow spreading from the North Pole in the distance to light up Forever.

As it passed them, the very air brightened, and soon the city was awash in daylight. Below his window, citizens flooded into the streets, cheering as light and life returned to the world.

Fen reached up to touch Lewin's cheek. "Looks like you might be stuck with me after all."

In response, Lewin kissed him again. Hard.

In the back of Fen's mind, a cheery voice whispered. *Hello, Fen, I'm Aris. The new world-mind.*

Fen's eyes widened and he let go of Lewin. *You do exist.* His mother had been right all along.

Yes. I have a lot to learn. I hope you'll help teach me about this world I've been born into. There are only a few liminals left in your generation who can hear me.

"Sure." He didn't realize he'd spoken aloud until Lewin raised an eyebrow.

"Everything okay, Fen?"

Fen grinned. He finally knew who *and* what he was.

He took Lewin's hand and pulled him back down onto the bed "Yeah, for the first time in a long time, I think it's going to be."

About Lamplighter

I originally wrote "Lamplighter" back in the 1990's. It was an offshoot of my first (unpublished) Liminal Fiction book, On a Shoreless Sea—not to be confused with The Shoreless Sea.

This one languished in my writer drawer for a couple decades until I pulled it out last year and reworked it, polishing it up and submitting it to the short story spec fic markets.

It's also a taste of the stories to come when I finally write the "middle trilogy" that will connect the Ariadne Cycle with the Oberon Cycle.

PROLEPSIS

Ian had been right about everything. Well, everything that *mattered* over the last thirty-nine years, since that autumn in 1986.

I stare at the pink envelope icon from I.H. Tragitto in my email.

I still don't know *how* he did it. *Could this really be from him?*

I tremble as I open it. A handwritten letter in Ian's neat script fills my floating screen…

AT TWENTY-SIX, I was a brand-new editor for the *Prolepsis* 'zine—its first gay one, though my boss didn't know it yet. I'd made my way up through the ranks of slush pile readers at other magazines, cultivating a keen editorial eye for the unexpected.

Called *Prolepsis*—the representation of a thing as existing before it actually does—the 'zine was fresh, edgy and new. We specialized in stories by authors who pushed the envelope, and none did that as well as I.H. Tragitto.

The world was a radically different place back then. There was no internet, no Facebook, no email, and no cell phones. You carried quarters in the pocket of your acid-washed jeans or parachute pants to make calls at *pay phones...* crazy, right?

Prolepsis didn't pay much—ten dollars a story—and they paid their star editor even less. I didn't care. I got to read cutting edge sci-fi before anyone else.

Tucson was a cow town. I would stop by the post office on Oracle on my way home from my job at Waldenbooks, to pick up the latest batch of stories that authors had snail-mailed to the magazine. We didn't call it snail mail back then. It was just *the mail,* though it still drove people crazy. *Going postal* was totally a thing.

One hot fall day, I.H.'s first story arrived in a bright pink envelope. I pulled it out of the box and snorted. *Authors. Always with the cheap tricks and gimmicks.* An envelope filled with glitter that "represented the stars." One printed entirely in the illegible *Lazer 84* font. And personal appeals based on an interview I'd done in *Omni Magazine*:

"You said you liked *Tron,* so you'll like this too. It has people living inside a giant computer..." I liked the *special effects* in Tron, but the movie was dreck.

I almost threw the pink envelope in the trash. Something stopped me, and it changed the course of my life.

I glanced over my shoulder to see if Jason was working the counter. He was cute—short, dark hair, with these piercing blue eyes and an ass I admired every time he bent over to pick up a package. He was about my age and made my gaydar *ping* off the charts. And talk about a *package...*

Our eyes met. He gave me a shy grin before turning back to his current customer.

I bit my lip. I was chickenshit at pick-ups. One day, maybe I'd find the courage to *talk to him* about more than the price of stamps and the renewal of the *Prolepsis* PO Box.

I stuck the envelopes under my arm and slipped out.

Donny was home, making out with his girlfriend Cindy in their room, right next to mine. "Donny, oh Donny!" reverberated through the little apartment.

I rolled my eyes. *Straight people.*

It was hot too… Tucson in August, and the air conditioner cost a mint to run. We were lucky to have one—most folks in town had a swamp cooler that didn't work worth crap in the muggy monsoon months.

I growled as I popped open a Jolt Cola—"all the sugar and twice the caffeine!"—and retreated to my bedroom, taking the latest batch of stories. I slipped on my headphones—big ones that covered your ears, with a long, curly cord. I jumped on my bed and put on my latest mix tape on my walkman.

These Dreams came on. I settled into the dreamlike intensity that only Heart could manage and started to read.

There were six stories in my mail that day. Why I remember that, I couldn't tell you, but I saved the pink envelope for last.

They were all so *already done*… first contact by lizard people a la *V*, flying space dragons like Pern, and even one that had come up with a "fourth" law of robotics, which got my attention until I realized it was just a blanket repudiation of the first three that let a robot do whatever it wanted.

Asimov would roll over in his grave, if he weren't still very much alive in the Upper West Side of Manhattan.

That left the pink envelope.

I picked it up reluctantly. I opened it with my shiny newish brass unicorn letter opener, the one I'd picked up at the Salvation

Army for a quarter. You can really score at the thrift shops if you dig deep, and on my salary, I had to stretch every last dollar.

The query letter was simple and succinct. *Points for that.*

Attn: Sean Miller
Prolepsis'Zine

Please find enclosed my short story "Firetime." I hope you enjoy it. I realize some elements may seem shocking in this time, but sci-fi is the art of the possible, and I assure you, these things are all possible.

Sincerely,
I.H. Tragitto

Intrigued, I pulled out the enclosed pages and began to read. *It was a time of fire and plague…*

I read through the whole story without noticing what was playing on my Walkman, forgetting about the heat and the carnal noises from the room next door, yanked into his world of the not-so-distant future. It was bold and frightening and so well drawn, the worldbuilding masterful. But that's not what struck me the most.

The protagonist was openly gay.

I'd never read anything like it.

Sure, McCaffrey flirted with the whole green dragon rider thing. And Lynn's The Dancers of Arun had nearly made me cream my pants. There were a few others… Delaney, LeGuin…

This went further. To imagine a world, even one in the midst of such chaos, where being gay was such a *normal* thing…

By the end of it, I was crying.

I pulled off my headphones and just stared at my closet door. I know, a little heavy on the metaphor. But something inside me had shifted.

The protagonist—James Cox—had a husband.

It was absurd on the face of it—even the *idea* of marrying another man was so beyond the pale, I couldn't see the pale. Whatever a pale was. That world was as far away from mine as Alpha Centauri was from Earth. *I want to go there.*

The 'zine owner wanted cutting edge, right? I would give it to him.

I pulled out a Xerox copy of my acceptance letter and contract from my old filing cabinet and filled in the blanks. I sealed up the envelope and licked a stamp to stick on it and put it on my desk to take out for the mail.

I had no idea what my decision would unleash.

That night I dreamed of a strange and compelling future, where Jason and I got married on a beach in Hawaii in matching tuxes.

Life went on.

I couldn't get Tragitto off my mind. Who was he? The address was a PO Box in Trenton, New Jersey—a long way away from Tucson. I wondered if being *out* there was easier than in a small desert town like Tucson.

I called a few of my editor friends, but none of them had ever received a bright-pink envelope or heard the author's name.

The contract came back a week later, to the day. It spelled out his full name as Ian Herbert Tragitto. I scratched my head… Tragitto sounded Italian, but Ian Herbert certainly didn't.

I wished this *world wide web* of his really existed—a magical place where I could type in a few words and find out everything about him.

I had friend in Levittown, Pennsylvania, just across the river from Trenton—Barry Finkleman—we'd gone to college together. He probably had a Trenton phone book. I called him and left a message on his answering machine.

I know—it was a little crazy. But I couldn't get Ian's story out of my head. The best science fiction is like that. It leaves you thinking about it for days and days.

I filed the contract and logged onto CompuServe to find the SciFiComm board. I left a message to see if anyone else had heard of Tragitto.

Then I went to the kitchen to make myself a bologna sandwich with a side of Cheetos.

A WEEK LATER, I got a frantic call from my copy editor. "You can't run this."

"Hey, Joel, calm down. What's up?" It was just after ten PM, standard work hours for the 'zine.

"It's… filth!"

I sighed. I knew what was coming, but I hadn't expected it from Joel. "What do you mean?"

"There's a couple fucking *faggots* in this thing."

"Ah, 'Firetime'? I reached across my desk and opened the window. Cool desert air poured in, fresh with the creosote smell that portended rain.

"Yes. You *can't* run this. We'll lose all of our readers."

I took a deep breath. "It's the *future*, Joel. Things are going to be different."

"Yeah, I get that. Give me lasers and Dyson spheres and warp drives any day. But this—"

"You didn't have a problem with that story with the harem last month."

"Th-That's different. That was *man heaven…*"

I shook my head. I'd been tempted to kick that one back, but the story itself had been *so good.* "Joel, do you *know* anyone who's gay?"

"Of course not. I don't hang out with perverts."

I winced. *If you only knew.*

"You're not one of those homosexuals, right Sean?" His suspicion was palpable.

"Of course not." It came out reflexively, but saying it took a little of my soul away. "I just think it's important to keep an open mind…"

"Sorry. It's disgusting—I won't do it. Find yourself another copy editor" He slammed the phone down, and I jumped in my seat.

"Fuuuuck." Joel was the best I'd found, and he was cheap—he lived in Kansas, for God's sake..

I'd just have to do it myself.

I logged on to CompuServe and checked my messages. There was a reply from a user named NotMyFault:

Contact me. I might know something about I.H. Tragitto. Tell me why you want to know.

I sat back and stared at the screen. I had no idea who this stranger was, but he didn't know who I was either.

I closed my eyes. Maybe I *should* tell someone. Just one person. It was relevant to my question, after all. Why not a random stranger who didn't know me from Adam?

I started with a tease.

I'm an editor for a sci-fi magazine It's about an author who sent me a story with certain… sensitive content. Just trying to find out more about him.

After a couple minutes' consideration, heart pounding in my chest, I sent the message and logged off.

THE ISSUE WAS off to the typesetter the next time I checked SciFiComm.

It was a good one, with four strong stories and an interview with Joe Haldeman. I'd had to pull an all-nighter on the editing, but that's what Jolt Cola's for, right?

I slept in until almost two PM the next day.

My mystery writer had returned his edits promptly—he must have done them the same day he got them.

I logged on to CompuServe. There was a message from my new friend.

I don't know if it helps, but I.H. Tragitto is a D&D character. I wrote a couple short stories about him. The name's a play on H.G Wells… I and H are the next letters, and Tragitto is Italian for a journey. Not sure how someone else would come up with the same name. Weird, Right? Have you ever been to San Francisco?

I stared at the screen as my mind tried to follow two paths simultaneously. One led to my mysterious author—what were the odds that he would independently come up with the same name?

The other led me to the person behind NotMyFault. I had no idea if they were male or female, gay or straight. Still, asking about San Francisco was odd. It was like the old dropping-the-matchbook thing… was he clueing me into the fact that he was gay? Then again, he had no idea of *my* sex or orientation either.

I took a deep breath. Someday things would change. The story told me so, and it felt right. Maybe I *needed* it to be right. But that future had to start somewhere.

I typed my reply. *Interesting. Did you ever share those stories anywhere? I'm in Tucson. Oh, and I'm gay.*

I sent it before I could stop myself, and then second-guessed myself for three days.

In the meantime, a new pink envelope arrived. I pulled it out of the box and stared at it for a minute, wondering what wonders it held inside.

I glanced at the mail counter. Jason was there, talking with an older woman with a cane and a little chihuahua on a leash.

I needed stamps, and the wait was short. I tucked the mail under my arm and got in line, running a hand through my hair. Hopefully I'd get Jason and not Lucy, the talkative blond, middle aged southern woman who always called me "hon" and "sweetie," and who smelled like cigars.

No such luck. Chihuahua lady pulled out her checkbook, her hand shaking as she reached for the pen on its chain.

I sighed as Lucy called me up.

"What can I do for ya, hon?"

"Sheet of stamps, please." My gaze strayed over to Jason. He rolled his eyes at me and I grinned.

"Rugs, fish, art or explorers?"

"What?" My attention snapped back to Lucy.

"We've got Indian Rugs, American Fish, Folk Art, and Arctic Explorers." She slapped them down in front of me. "Pick your poison, sweetie."

"Um…" None of them looked particularly appealing. "How about explorers?" At least they were ruggedly handsome, like the Brawny paper towel guy. I'd had a crush on him since they'd introduced him when I was in junior high.

"Sure. That'll be eleven dollars for a sheet of 50."

"Perfect." I pulled out my *Prolepsis* account check book.

She rang up the stamps. "How's that little newspaper of yours doing?"

I frowned. "The *'zine* is doing great." I ripped out the check and handed it over with my driver's license and recorded the amount in the register.

"What's it about?" Jason's voice this time.

I looked up, grinning.

Ms. Chihuahua had left the counter, and I was the last customer in the room. "Sci-fi and fantasy."

Lucy frowned. "I never liked that much. My son Jimmy loves it, though.... What's that old show called? Star Truck?"

"*Star Trek*." Jason winked at me. "I *love* sci-fi. I heard they're working on a new Trek series."

I stared at him. "You're a Trekkie?"

"*Trekker*." He gave me a once-over. "We should watch it together sometime."

My heart hammered in my chest and my throat went dry. "I'd like that," I managed finally, swallowing hard.

"Here you go." Lucy handed me the stamps and my ID.

"It's a date." Jason locked his drawer. "Gonna take my break, Lucy. Can you handle the crowd?"

She looked around the empty room and laughed. "Yeah, I think I can manage."

Then he was gone.

I stared at his empty station and realized we hadn't chosen a day. Still, I couldn't help but whistle all the way home. *He asked me out!*

~

I SAVED Ian's new story for the next day. It's like the delayed orgasm thing—the pleasure really *is* more intense if you wait a bit between rounds.

Waldenbooks was busy that day, and it wasn't until afternoon that I had a few minutes of peace and quiet. I browsed the sci-fi and fantasy section, looking for something, *anything* gay. I spent a fair chunk of my income with my bookstore discount, but my bookshelf was running out of room and the rent was due. Still, Tragitto's story was always on my mind, and I wondered why there weren't more like it.

I found nothing.

I'd have to visit Antigone books over the weekend for my fix. Kate would have something for me.

I stopped by the Wherehouse on the way home, craving *something* about people like me. I spent half an hour reading VHS covers, looking for "Johnny had a special friend."

Seriously, that was how you knew it had gay content back then. Gay content in the eighties was super coded. Sure, you could mail-order porn, but for actual fiction, you had to be good at reading between the lines.

Some production companies, like Merchant Ivory, could be counted on too, but gay films and books, especially sci-fi, were still few and far between.

I settled on *My Beautiful Laundrette.* Daniel Day-Lewis was so gorgeous back then.

The clerk looked like a high school jock, arms as thick as saguaros. "Want any candy with that, *faggot*?" He whispered the last word, staring at me to make sure I'd heard it.

"No. Thanks." I kicked myself for thanking the asshole, but I'd learned the lesson the hard way in high school. *Blend in. Don't fight back. Avoid trouble.*

He grinned and handed me the video and my card. "Have a nice day, faggot." This time he didn't bother to whisper.

I left the store, shaken. I'd have to cancel my membership—no way was I going through that abuse again. Besides, there was a Blockbuster close by that would be happy to have my business.

Still, I felt craven.

It was raining, so I dashed past the ocotillos to my Volkswagen Bug—the poor car was older than I was—and slammed the door behind me, cranking open the heat vent on the floor.

I drove through the heavy monsoon rain, thrilled that fall was finally coming. As luck would have it, I found a spot not too far from the apartment. I dashed up the stairs, getting soaked in the process.

My roommates were out, so I had the living room to myself.

Outside the sliding glass door that led to our balcony, the rain fell hard, and the sky thundered. Inside, I was cozy and dry.

I made some ramen with a bit of frozen broccoli and a Jolt Cola for dinner and settled in for a couple hours in another world.

When it was over, I retreated to my room and opened the pink envelope.

Dear Sean,

I'm glad you enjoyed my first story. Enclosed, please find another —The Seventh Gender. Please know how much it means to me that you published "Firetime." My teenaged self would have loved to read something like that.

I know it must be hard to be in the closet, but take heart. It gets better. One day you will find the strength to come out, and your life will change forever.

Best,

—Ian

I stared at the letter, dumbfounded. How did he know I was closeted? Let alone gay? I wasn't out to anyone I knew, not even Donny and Cindy.

I frowned and pulled out the story. The text was clean and crisp… probably one of the new laser printers. It put my old Epson dot matrix to shame.

I settled in on my bed, pulling my *Star Wars* comforter up over my knees, and began to read.

By the time I was done, my eyes were wet, and my brain hurt. Tragitto's new story had multiple genders—people who were "gender fluid" and some who were "gender queer"—I was still unclear on that one. And even folks who were "non-binary," with no gender at all.

I was familiar with "transgender"—everyone knew about Christine Jorgensen—but the world Tragitto painted showed such a rich variety of gender expression that it confounded me. It took me a bit to get used to the pronouns "they/them/theirs" for one of the characters, but soon enough that faded into invisibility. The last line, "They are who they are, and no one else can take that from them," stuck with me.

I sat back and stared at the final page, thinking about what it would mean to come out. And then I realized I already had. With NotMyFault.

I logged in eagerly to see if they had replied. There was a message waiting for me.

I'm gay too. I don't know anyone else who is. I live in a little town in Pennsylvania where they beat the shit out of anyone who's different, but I want to move to San Francisco—or maybe New York—when I graduate from high school.

My heart beat faster. *He's gay, too.*

Then I frowned. I was a gay man talking to a minor. I could get into all sorts of trouble for that if his parents ever found out. I logged out without replying and shut down the computer.

Still, something in me had shifted. I had come out to someone, and he'd returned the favor. Someone in the world knew I was gay and didn't care.

I closed my eyes and imagined what my mysterious writer friend might be like. Would Tragitto be dark, mysterious, handsome, and kind? Italian, so dark hair and swarthy skin…

I locked my bedroom door, laid back on my bed and pulled out a Kleenex.

When I was done, I washed my hands and filled out a new contract, licking and slapping an *arctic explorer* stamp on it to send it out in the morning. I figured he'd like that.

MY PHONE RANG, that shrill knock-your-socks-off middle-of-the-night ring everyone dreads.

I opened my eyes, staring blearily at the red numbers on the alarm clock. Three-thirty in the morning. Who would call in the middle of the night?

My sister Carrie. *Oh God, something must have happened.*

Donny banged on the wall. "Sean, pick up the damned phone!"

"Sorry!" I stumbled across the carpeted floor and grabbed the receiver before the fourth ring. "Hello?"

"What the hell did you do?" Ed Longfellow was as angry as I'd ever heard him.

"Ed, it's not even dawn here yet." The call from the UK must be costing him a mint.

"Sorry. I always forget." He growled. "I just got the latest issue of the 'zine."

Ah. "I'm really proud of this one. Some great stories—"

"Don't try to bullshit me. What were you thinking with this 'Firetime' story?"

"What do you mean?" My heart sunk. I knew *exactly* what he meant, but I wanted him to say it.

"This bloody *Nancy boy* bullshit is going to get us boycotted in half the shops in England, not to mention the US and Canada. What were you thinking?"

I took a deep breath. "Ed, you told me when you hired me that I had full editorial autonomy." I kept my voice calm.

"That's because I thought you had sense not to pull bollocks like this." There was a pregnant pause. "Sean, you're not queer, are you?"

"Of course not." The speed with which it came out again shocked me. I felt like Peter denouncing Christ. Here I was, publishing this story to help gay youth, and I couldn't even tell my own boss I was one of them.

Disgusted with myself, I plowed ahead, trying to salvage things. "Just think how many gay men there are out there. What an untapped market this could be? No one speaks to them, speaks for them."

"We're certainly not going to either. Pull the issue."

I ran a hand through my hair. "It's too late. It's already out in all the stores. You know that… you guys are the last to get them."

There was a long silence.

"Ed?"

"Let me think about it. I'll call you later this afternoon. If you pull this kind of bollocks again—"

I bit my lip. *I already had.* But of course I didn't tell him that. "Understood."

He hung up without another word.

I set down the receiver and went back to bed.

I stared at the ceiling, seething. At Ed for calling people like me "Nancy boys." At myself, for being too chickenshit to object. And at Ian fucking Tragitto for getting me into this position in the first place.

Then I had an idea.

It was foolhardy and reckless. I rejected it out of hand, at first. But it stuck with me, worming its way into my brain the way those midnight ideas do. I tossed and turned, breaking into a cold sweat. I'd have to wash the sheets in the morning.

When the sun rose, I'd made up my mind.

I pulled out one of the pink envelopes to double check Ian's address, and wrote out a letter, sealing it and dropping it off in the mailbox on the way to work. Coincidentally, my copy of the Advocate was in my box, in its brown paper envelope.

I stared at it for a long moment. *Talk about metaphors.* So many of us hid who we were behind bland wrappers. And people like Ed just assumed we were *normal,* like them.

Fuck that. I didn't want to be normal if it meant hiding for the rest of my life. "Firetime" had shaken me to my core, revealing shocking new possibilities, and that couldn't be undone.

I felt like dancing.

"Firetime" did stir up a few protests, but in the end only one bookstore—a hole-in-the-wall in Kansas—cancelled their subscription over it. Maybe the world wasn't quite as homophobic a I'd feared.

There was the cute guy on that show *Brothers*—I may have gone through an entire box of Kleenex over him—and even *Cagney & Lacey* and *The Golden Girls* had gay and lesbian characters now.

A few weeks had passed since I'd last logged onto CompuServe. I'd been avoiding NotMyFault, afraid of being labeled a pedophile or worse. But I'd also been thinking about my own high school years as a closeted teen.

What if he didn't have anyone else? My silence might be deafening, and if anything happened to him… I couldn't have that on my conscience.

There were six messages waiting for me from NotMyFault—all variations of *Are you there?* Except for the last one.

Sorry to have bothered you. I won't bug you anymore.

I sighed. *Poor kid.* I sent him a quick message. *Last time,* I promised myself.

Hey Not… sorry, it's been a rough couple of weeks. I just wanted you to know something, I'm the editor of a sci-fi 'zine called Prolepsis. You're going to want to get a copy of the next issue. And remember to be proud of who you are. There's nothing *wrong with you.*

Yeah, I was aware of the irony.

Then, remembering what Ian had written to me, I added *It gets better.*

I signed off and went to work. As I was unpacking books, I found a copy of *Worlds Apart: An Anthology of Lesbian and Gay Science Fiction and Fantasy*. I hugged it to my chest, grinning. It felt like a sign. *The Universe has spoken.*

On the way home, I stopped by the post office. My box had a yellow slip, so I went to the counter to pick up my package.

It was a pink envelope, like the others but stuffed to the gills. Jason handed it over to me, his hand touching mine briefly. "Here you go."

I adjusted my glasses, blushing. "Thanks." I turned to go, but something stopped me. I was sick of hiding. "Hey, want to come over to my place this weekend? My roomies are out of town, and *TBS* is running a Trek marathon…"

"Sure!" Jason grinned, lighting up my heart. "I can bring some Jiffy Pop."

I laughed. I hadn't made any of the stove-top popcorn since I was a kid. "That'd be great. Five o'clock?" I scribbled my address down on the back of a piece of junk mail.

Jason nodded. "See you then." He tucked it into his back pocket, and I got another look at his beautiful ass. I squirmed, adjusting myself on the way out the door and grinning like an idiot.

My good mood evaporated the minute I walked into the apartment.

Donny was standing in the living room, leafing through a copy of the Advocate, frowning.

At least he didn't find my porn stash. I set the mail on the entry table, my heart in my throat.

Donny turned to stare at me. "I needed an extension cord, so I went into your room to borrow one, and found this." He held it out toward me.

"Yeah." What would he do? Beat me up? Kick me out? I mean, we were both on the lease, but still…

"Are you gay?"

That frog in my throat evaporated, taking all the moisture with it. Incongruously, I thought about Peter in the Bible again. *Third time.* "I'm… I… Yeah." *Not my finest moment, but still.* I'd said it. I closed my eyes and braced myself for his anger.

"What the fuck, Sean? Why didn't you just tell me?"

"What?" I opened my eyes to stare at him blankly. "You're not angry?"

"Hell yes, I'm angry. You kept this from me. Why? You didn't trust me enough to tell me."

I collapsed onto the orange floral print couch we'd gotten from a friend—so long we'd had to push it up over the second-floor balcony to get it into the apartment because we couldn't get it around the entryway corner. "I thought you'd beat the crap out of me. Or throw me out. Or something just as bad."

Donny sat next to me, shaking his head. "Dude, my uncle's gay."

"I know. And you always say shit about him—"

Donny barked a laugh. "Because he's an asshole. But once you get past that, he's cool enough."

We sat in silence for a minute, staring at the sliding glass door together.

"So you're *not* gonna beat the shit out of me?"

"Dude." Donny laughed. "Wait until I tell Cindy. She said you were when she first moved in, but I said no. Guess my gaydar sucks, huh?"

I gave Donny an appraising look. He was deeper than I gave him credit for. "So if I have a date over on Saturday night…."

"Score!" His nose wrinkled. "If you guys do it, though, just keep it quiet, okay?"

I laughed. "Like you and Cindy?"

"That's different—" Our eyes met, and he must have read the look on my face. "Okay, fair. Maybe just tell me first, and I'll clear out with Cindy?"

I nodded. "Deal."

And just like that, I was out of the closet.

Of course, it wasn't that easy. Coming out isn't an event—it's a never-ending process. Every day you decide to come out or to stay in with every new situation. Do you say "my boyfriend" or "we"

when you tell a co-worker what you did last weekend? Do you drop your voice an octave when talking with a really macho customer?

That night I read through the new stories Ian had sent me. They were a window on a whole different world—kinda the point, I know—and they were everything I'd asked for. He had a real talent for social sci-fi, peering into the murky future and pulling out what *queer* possibilities that went way beyond the gay and lesbian community as I knew it.

There was one about a bisexual woman who became the governor of the moon colony of New Oregon.

Another story which featured a hermaphrodite. It had a purple post-it attached—never saw one of those before—explaining that the term *intersex* was preferred in the community.

I wondered what Trenton was like—it must be some kind of queer utopia. I swore to myself that one day I'd visit there and meet Mr. Tragitto.

There were more in the envelope waiting for me, and each one was a little gem of queer awesomeness.

Ed was going to blow his top, and I'd surely be fired. But when I thought about my own high school days, and about NotMyFault, I knew it was worth it.

On Saturday night, Jason arrived right on time with the promised Jiffy Pop. He was adorable in his white high tops, with his collar of his pink Izod shirt pulled up around his neck over a turquoise blue t-shirt. We kissed cheeks and I felt very European.

I'd prepared a gourmet meal—Stouffers Lasagna—and the aroma filled the apartment.

"That smells good." Jason sat at the table.

"Give me a sec. It's just about ready." I'd never actually come out to Jason. I'd just assumed this was a date, but was he on the same page? So I'd devised a plan. Not a very complicated one, but short notice and all that, right?

I served him a heaping slice of lasagna. "What do you want to drink?"

"Got any wine coolers?"

I grinned. "Man after my own heart." I popped open a couple of Bartles and James and slipped into my chair. "Here you go."

Jason took a swig, his eyes twinkling.

I took my chance. "I just came out to my roommate this week." I said it as casually as I could, though my heart was hammering in my chest. See? Not much of a plan.

Jason's eyes went wide. "Holy shit. How did it go?"

Good sign. "He was pissed at me. Asked me why I didn't tell him sooner. Then he was totally cool with it."

Jason nodded. "People surprise you sometimes."

I took a bite of my lasagna.

"My dad threw me out of the house when I came out."

I bit my lip. *Bingo.*

"Mom came after me, and when she found me at Alex Tanner's house, she sent me to stay with my Aunt Gloria. She was pissed too —at my Dad. A week later, I moved back home." He shrugged. "He's still a bit weird about it—goes all quiet whenever I mention anything gay."

I laughed. I felt good. No, *great*. Better than I had in years. "I'm sure he'll come around."

"I hope so. How about you? How did your folks take it?" He took a swig and sat back, looking at me with those beautiful blue eyes.

"I lost them years ago." The pain was old, and familiar. "My sister doesn't know I'm gay."

"I'm so sorry." His gaze pierced me. "I figured you for a closet case. But I'm glad you're doing it. You don't know how much weight you're carrying until you let it go."

I could get lost in those eyes.

His hand strayed to his crotch. "You know I didn't really come here for a trek marathon, right? I mean, I love the show, but..." He looked around. "You said your roommates are gone for the weekend?"

"Yeah, we have the place to ourselves." My heart went into overdrive.

Jason grinned. "I brought protection." Then he was next to me, his lips on mine, and I decided I didn't care if dinner got cold.

I LAY BESIDE JASON, a little sticky and a little sore, but I didn't care. I was flying.

I was glad he'd brought a condom, too. That AIDS thing was scary as shit.

"I've been thinking about this for months." His eyes met mine across the pillow, and a lazy smile slid across his face.

"Really? Me too." All that time, watching him from afar, and he'd been watching me too.

"I would get excited whenever you came in to check your box." He leaned in and kissed me, and sat up, displaying his beautiful chest. He was sticky too.

Gotta wash the damned sheets again. "I was checking out your box too." It should have been sexy, but it just came out… weird.

Jason groaned. "Seriously?" He turned over and looked around the room. "Nice apartment." He picked up the pile of papers from my nightstand. "What are these?"

I sat up too, propping my head on my hands. "Those are for the next issue of Prolepsis."

"Your 'zine?"

"You *do* listen." I grinned.

He laughed, a beautiful, whole-hearted sound that made me like him even more. "To you? Always. What are they about?"

I hesitated. If there was anyone I could tell, it was Jason. "It's our first—and probably last—all queer issue."

Jason stared at me. "Holy shit, are you kidding me?"

"No. They're by this amazing writer. But the last time I published one of his stories, my boss went apeshit and basically threatened to fire me if I did it again, so…"

"You *have* to do it. Oh my god, if I had read something like that as a teen…"

"I know." More points in the Jason column.

"What are you doing for cover art?"

I shrugged. "I don't know. Something simple. A pink triangle? I don't want Ed getting wind of this before it's out, and I'm not sure if our usual artist is gay friendly."

"I'll do it." He was scanning the pages raptly. Then he blushed. "If you'll let me."

"What?"

"I'm a graphic artist. I've been taking classes." He laughed at the confused expression on my face. "What, you didn't think I wanted to stay at the post office forever? My dad got me that job. Though the benefits are pretty damned good."

"That would be amazing." It felt like fate. "I'll make you copies so you can see what it's all about."

Dinner was getting cold in the kitchen, but I decided it could wait. "Want to go again?"

Jason laughed. "Yes, please." He set down the stack of papers and practically leapt at me across the bed.

We never did get to the lasagna.

Three weeks later, the issue finally arrived. I dropped the box on the bed. "You guys ready?"

Donny appeared at the doorway. "You're a real drama queen, you know."

I laughed. "You're learning fast. I approve. Where's Jason?"

"Coming!" He squeezed past Donny to stand by me. We'd spent nearly every night together, working and getting to know one another, and he'd put almost as much work into this damned thing as I had.

There was a loud pop from the living room.

I frowned. "What's that?"

Cindy appeared at the door, carrying a tray and four plastic champagne glasses. "I thought this celebration needed a little bubbly."

I laughed. "Where'd you get that?"

"Safeway had a special. It's imported!" She poured them each a glass. "To queerness!"

I held mine up. "To queerness." The change in them since I'd come out had been nothing short of revolutionary.

I was almost ready to tell my sister, knowing that I had support if it went off a cliff.

Ian had been right.

"You guys ready?" I held the box cutter in the air like a magic wand.

"Just do it already." Jason put a hand on my shoulder, and I felt warm all over.

I slid the razor-edge across the packing tape and pried the box open, removing the protective paper, and pulled out a copy of *Prolepsis*.

Donny choked.

I stared at him, worried that this was a bridge too far.

"Dude, that's the gayest thing I have ever seen." He looked at me. "And I live with you."

I burst out laughing, my doubts and fears fleeing. Sure, we'd be banned from a few places, and yeah, I'd probably get fired. But it was worth it for those queer kids out there who would finally see themselves in our stories.

Donny was right, though. The cover practically sparkled with rainbow colors, and emblazoned under the logo over a hot pink triangle, it said: *The Queer Issue.*

"Are you *finally* going to read the foreword to us?" Jason peered over my shoulder.

I'd kept it under wraps, not ready to share it with anyone, but now the whole world would see it. "Sure." I flipped it open and began to read.

A friend of mine once told me how much it would have meant to read about a gay character in a sci-fi story.

For twenty-five years, I have lived my life in the closet, rarely seeing anyone like me reflected in popular media, let-alone sci-fi. The few gay characters in SFF are inevitably naked stereotypes, and many of them live with a sense of shame, or are killed off like they don't matter.

In one recent film, the main character came out after a rousing round of sex in a parking lot (because of course, we gays never *have sex indoors) and the shame of it killed his father and caused his mother to send him to therapy to wish away the gay.*

I'm sick of it, and so I'm doing something about it.

I am a proud, out gay man with a beautiful partner, and friends who love me. And by chance, I have been given an opportunity to finally make that dream come true for hundreds, maybe even thousands of queer folks—lesbian, gay, bisexual, transgender, and beyond.

What do I mean by beyond*?*

Read these stories and see.

They have kindled a dream in me of a more equal world, a place that, for all its warts and flaws, will treat me the same as it treats my straight friends.

It's a dream worth fighting for.

I glanced up at my friends.

Even Donny had a tear in his eye. "That's beautiful, dude."

Cindy squeezed his arm and nodded, wiping her eyes with the edge of her shirt.

"I'm proud of you," Jason kissed me, and my roommates retreated, leaving us to ourselves.

"The cover's amazing. Donny's right, it practically *screams* gay."

"Thanks." Jason grinned and kissed me, hard. "I'll make you scream…" he whispered in my ear.

I moved the box off the bed. "One sec." I leaned out the door. "Donny…"

"I know, dude." He flashed me the thumbs-up. "We're heading out to grab something at Mickie D's. Back in an hour."

The door slammed, and I laughed.

An hour would be just about right.

THE OTHER SHOE dropped a week later.

The phone rang, this time waiting politely until just after eight AM. "Morning, Ed."

"What in the bloody hell, Sean?"

I took a deep breath and tried again. "*Good morning*, Ed."

"Yeah, good *goddamned* morning to you too. I've been getting calls all morning about this new issue. *What did you do?*"

Jason sat up in bed, rubbing his eyes. "Who is it?"

I motioned him to silence. "Did you get your copy yet?"

"No. It's running late. Probably a customs thing…"

"Call me back when you do." I hung up the phone, as shocked at myself as he probably was. Still, Ed didn't pay me enough to treat me like shit.

The phone rang again.

I picked it up. "Ed, I said to call me when—"

"Mr. Miller?"

I frowned. "Yes?"

"This is Devin Taylor from the Advocate. Are you familiar with the magazine?"

My mouth went dry. "Yeah. I'm a subscriber."

Devin's voice brightened. "Oh, that's awesome. I'd like to ask you a few questions about the latest issue of *Prolepsis*. I just got a copy, and it's… damn. It's something."

I grinned, covering the phone receiver. "It's someone from the Advocate."

Jason's eyes went wide, and he slipped out of bed, giving me an amazing view of his backside as he pulled on his underwear.

"I have the cover artist here with me too… should I get him on the line?"

Jason shook his head, mouthing *No!*

"That would be great." There was a pause. "Are you two…?"

"He'd be happy to. And yes. For three weeks now." I covered the phone again. "Go pick up the phone in the kitchen. He wants to talk with us both."

Jason sighed. He shrugged on his shirt and pants, flashing me his best *I'm going to make you pay for this later* look and made his way to the kitchen. "Jason Kelley here."

We talked with Devin for an hour, and only when we hung up did it hit me. I'd just come out to a national magazine, one with far more reach than our own little 'zine.

Jason appeared at the doorway. "Wow, that was intense." He frowned. "You okay?"

I shook my head, shaking. "What the hell am I doing?"

Jason was at my side in an instant. "What's going on?"

"I think I just came out to *everyone*."

Jason laughed. "Yeah, I think you're right. How will your sister take it?"

My parents were gone—car accident when I was seventeen. My sister Carrie was four years older than me, and she'd taken care of me ever since. "Well, she's Catholic…"

Jason nodded. "You should call her."

"Yeah." I picked up the phone.

"Want me to leave you alone? I could whip up some breakfast—"

"No. Please stay." I pulled him back down to the bed.

"Whatever happens, it'll be okay." He put his arm around my waist, his warmth bleeding through my shirt.

I took a deep breath and nodded. *I can do this.* "Okay." I dialed the phone. Carrie was married to a nice banker and lived in Connecticut. It was already after eleven there.

"Hello?" She sounded bored.

"Hey sis. It's Seaney." I ignored Jason's snort.

"Seaney!" Her squeal almost broke my ear. "Everything okay?"

"Yeah. Listen, you have a sec?" She always made time for me.

"Sure. What's up, little bro?"

"Remember that 'zine I work on?" I twisted the phone cord around my finger.

"*Prosthesis*?"

I laughed. "*Prolepsis*. We just released a special issue, and the national news media did an interview with me about it."

"That's amazing, Seaney! I knew you'd make it big."

"There's a catch."

Her voice got serious. "Tell me."

I hesitated.

Jason nodded, doing the *go on* gesture.

"Carrie, I'm gay." It came out in a rush, and my heart was beating fast in my chest and my face was flushed.

There was a long silence on the other end of the line.

"Carrie?"

"I *know*."

I frowned. *What the hell?* "What do you mean, you *know*?"

She laughed. "Come on, Sean. You weren't exactly an athletic child…"

I snorted. "Gays can be athletic."

"Maybe so. But you played with Barbies, and you always liked to wear mamma's shoes…" She trailed off.

I closed my eyes. I missed them too.

"Anyhow, I always figured you were, and that one day you'd tell me. When you were ready."

"So… it's okay?" I'd been bracing myself for this for weeks.

Carrie snorted too, like she used to when we were kids and I said something stupid. "Of course it's okay. You're my little brother."

I bit my knuckle to stop myself from crying. "I wish you were here, Sis."

"Gotta run, Seaney. Work meeting. But call me tonight. I want to hear all about it!"

"I will. Love you."

"Love you more."

I hung up the phone and stared at Jason. "She said she already knew. What the hell… does everyone *know*?"

Jason laughed. "Well, you're not exactly butch." He kissed me to take the sting out of it. "What time do you have to go to work?"

"Not until this afternoon."

"Good. We can celebrate again." He kissed my cheek. "Come on. I'll make us breakfast, I'm starving."

I followed him out of the room, feeling light as a feather.

I CRASHED BACK DOWN to earth two days later when Ed called me back.

"Hello Sean." He sounded tired.

"Good morning, Ed."

"You're fired, of course."

I sighed. I'd been expecting this, but still… "Good morning, Ed."

"Bollocks, Sean! I explicitly told you not to publish anything by this new writer again—"

"Actually, you said not to publish anything like 'Firetime' again. And in fairness, I didn't." I was baiting him. I knew I shouldn't, but I couldn't help it.

He growled. "That's *enough*, Sean. Do you know how many calls I've fielded from bookstores cancelling their standing orders?"

"Twenty?"

"Over a hundred. That's ten percent of our business, Sean."

"Queer folks need to see themselves in sci-fi."

"Then let them make their own 'zine. We're not in the business of catering to every poof, bender and shirt-lifter—"

I grinned in spite of myself. "You are now."

There was a long pause. "Sean, was I in any way unclear when we spoke last month?"

"No, Ed, you made your homophobia perfectly clear."

That shut him up.

I pushed ahead. "Last month, you asked if I was gay, and I lied to you. I'm sorry for that. I'm a proud gay man, and since apparently I don't work for you anymore, I don't see why I have to keep taking your *bloody bollocks*." I slammed down the receiver.

Donny appeared at the door. "Was that…?"

"Yeah. I just got eighty-sixed. Ironic, right?"

Donny nodded. "Yeah, I guess? Oh… the year." He laughed, then covered his mouth. "You okay?"

I didn't need toxic influences in my life. I managed a smile. "Yeah. I am."

Donny nodded. "You're a good guy, Sean. Even *with* the whole gay thing." He grinned.

"Backatcha, even with the whole *straight thing*."

Donny lifted his Coors in respect. "Toochay."

"It's *too-shay*, but keep working on it." I took a deep breath. "Thanks, Donny. I have a bit of wrap-up work to do on the magazine before work."

"I'll leave you to it."

I logged onto CompuServe and was happy to see a message from NotMyFault.

Thank you for the stories. I read the issue five times, in my room under my blanket with a flashlight. I didn't tell you before, but I almost killed myself last year. I didn't know there was anyone else like me. This morning, I told my mother, and she didn't throw me out. It kinda freaked her out, but I showed her your magazine, and she started to cry. You will never know what this meant to me.

I sat back and stared at the monitor. *That* made it all worth it. I typed a quick message back:

Always be true to yourself. I just came out to my sister, so I'm right there with you, pal.

Then I logged off and set about packing up all of the Prolepsis supplies to ship to whatever unlucky sucker Ed chose to hire to replace me.

MY WORLD WENT crazy for a couple weeks after the Advocate story. The local news had me on, and the queer issue was featured in both the New York Times and the San Francisco Chronicle.

I even went on Donahue, which flew me out to the Big Apple for the filming. The hotel accommodations were crappy, but I didn't care. It was New York City, a world away from Tucson. Donahue was way taller than I thought he'd be.

Jason came with me, and nobody cared.

With all the attention, I was offered a job at Tor in New York as a "diversity editor," whatever the hell that was. I took it—I'd start in a week, which set off a furious round of packing and goodbyes.

Surprisingly, Cindy and Donny were the hardest. They made me a straight sandwich, hugging me from both sides and squeezing me tight.

I asked Jason to come, and he surprised the hell out of me when he immediately said yes.

When the *Prolepsis* issue went back for a second printing and a third, I got a call from Ed at a respectable eleven-thirty in the morning.

"Good morning, Sean."

"Ed." I had half a mind to hang up on his sorry ass. I sank down on my bed.

"I've been giving things a lot of thought. I may have been a bit… rash when I fired you."

I snorted. "You seemed very sure at the time."

"I know. It's… I'm an old man, Sean. Change isn't easy for me."

I knew he was just calling me because I'd made him a bunch of money with the queer issue. I was well within my rights to tell him to take his stupid little 'zine and shove it up his… well, you get the picture.

But just because Ed was a small man didn't mean *I* had to be. "If you're calling to apologize, I accept."

There was a long pause. "Yes. I am. I'm sorry for what I said to you, Sean. I'd like you to come back to work for Prolepsis. I could even up your pay—"

"I appreciate that, Ed. I know how hard this must be for you." At my side, Jason was squirming. I waved him off. "I just accepted a position at Tor, so thank you, but I won't need that job back." I'd already given my notice at Waldenbooks.

"Ah." That long pause again. "Well, it was a pleasure working with you, Sean. Truly. Good luck to you." He hung up.

"You should have let him have it." Jason punched his fist into his palm. "After what he said to you?"

I laughed. "I know. But sometimes it's better to be the bigger man."

Jason kissed me, his eyebrow raised.

"Don't say it."

He laughed. "Without Ed, you'd never have gotten this new job—"

"I wouldn't say *never.* You sure you want to come with me?" We'd only been together for a month and a half. "It's a big change."

Jason took my hand. "I've been watching you for two years." He blushed. "I know that sounds kinda creepy, but it's true. I wanted to ask you out every day, but I was scared you'd say no." He looked into my eyes. "Of course I want to go. And come on, it's New York City, one of the gay capitals of the world!"

I squeezed his hand, wiping the tears away. "Just think how much gayer it will be when we get there?" I kissed him and felt that surge again. I pushed him back down on the bed, nuzzling his neck.

Packing up my own stuff could wait a little longer.

So here I am, a half century later. Hard to believe I made it to 2025, after all the troubles of the early twenty-twenties.

I did meet NotMyFault… a sweet kid named Daniel Allen, eight years younger than me, with an acne-scarred face and a smile that would win anyone over that was on full display the day we had lunch together at the Plaza. A meeting that would change my life, though I didn't know it until later.

I lost my beautiful Jason in '96 to AIDS.

Somehow I escaped the Great Plague, and the second one too, the one that turned New York City into a ghost town.

Tonight's my retirement party. I've had an amazing career spanning four publishers and hundreds of books filled with characters of every size, shape, and stripe, including a few of my own—a fitting legacy.

I still have a copy of that queer issue of Prolepsis framed behind me here in my office—the highlight of my career, even though the 'zine has long been consigned to the dustbin of history. Ian was right about almost everything, though he changed some of the details.

And now you're back. The mystery that has confounded me for fifty years.

I tremble as I open the pink envelope's pdf file on the translucent screen above my desk, and stare at his neat, handwritten script.

Dear Sean,

I read about your retirement in Locus… congrats to you on a long and illustrious career. By now, I've been revealed for the fraud that I am… less a science-fiction writer and more of a chronicler of that which has happened in the years since you received my first story, "Firetime."

A few details were changed, but the song remains the same. We never colonized the moon—not yet, anyhow.

I'm a physicist. I've been working on a space-time folding project… let's just call it a time machine… for a couple decades.

I've discovered a few things. While it is possible to send something through time, mass matters. The heavier the thing, the more power it takes. And living things don't make it through… still living.

I decided to do a test one day a couple years ago. Nothing big. I rented a PO box in Jersey City, just far enough away from where I live to avoid suspicion should something go wrong. I installed two prototypes of my device—one in my home box where the mailman picks up, and one at the post office.

I sent a letter from home to the owner of the PO box, a few decades earlier.

I'd chosen the letter recipient on purpose—a kid in Trenton who would later become a gay porn star. His name isn't important, but let's just say you've probably seen his ass more than once on film.

It took a lot of calibration to establish a rolling connection with that moment in time. I finally managed to get his attention with a letter in a pink envelope. He would send it back to me in my home box, and I would retrieve it and send him a new one. I ordered some vintage stamps for the purpose off of eBay, though I think I screwed up once and used a stamp from 1987. Still, that's why it's called an experiment, right?

Once we had established a relationship, I had an idea.

I grew up in the seventies and eighties, a lonely, nerdy kid. What if I wrote some stories about kids like me and got them published in the eighties? How would that change the world? And how would I know? Time travel paradoxes are a tricky business.

So I wrote a long summary of the world as I knew it then. I sent it to my eighties friend along with a new request—to forward a story called "Firetime" to you. It was set during the plague year, and from what I'd read of your illustrious career in publishing—yes, you still had one, even in the old timeline—you'd snap it right up.

By the way, in the old version of your life, you didn't come out until your forties.

My soon-to-be-actor friend was under strict orders to hold my other envelope, unopened—the one with the summary—for three months, and then send it back to me. My control group, so to speak. I paid him handsomely in pre-1986 cash—again, a challenge to get my hands on, but in the internet age, anything is possible.

You know most of the rest.

You're probably wondering about the name. When I was a kid, one of my best friends—Daniel, I think?—used it for his D&D character. I was even deeper in the closet than he was, but it stuck with me. It seemed appropriate, as the H.G. Wells of our time. Or maybe that's too immodest.

So much has changed in four decades. Which brings me back to the present.

When my friend sent back the sealed letter, I opened it eagerly, excited to find out what changes my meddling had wrought. It was a first-of-its-kind experiment, reaching across time to change the past for the better. Or at least I think it was. Who can say if someone else has tried this before?

I read my historical summary, my hands trembling like yours probably are now.
There were *changes. Most were minor, and I'm sure there were many beyond what I had managed to chronicle in my summary. But one stood out.*

In the old timeline, I'd had a partner, a man who spent his whole life with me. Seth was a gardener, a caretaker, with warm hands and a heart that had room for even those who hated him. That's all I know about him, because in this new timeline, he never existed—at least not for me. One of those forking changes sent him on a different path, and we never met.

I didn't know I was missing him until I read my own letter.

My career has been successful. I've risen to great heights, and yet somehow I still followed this same course. How? I don't know.
It haunts me. Maybe I was meant *to do this, no matter the consequences, large or small. Maybe it's my comeuppance for daring to challenge the gods of time and space.*

In any case, I drove back to Trenton and removed my devices the next day. I smashed them into little pieces with a hammer and deleted all my research. I'm done with time, and I suspect time will soon be done with me.
I have terminal cancer, one that even gene therapy can't cure.

Don't feel sorry for me. I lived a good life, and I helped others where I could. And please don't try to find me. I will deny all of this.

Still, I thought you deserved to know. Because of us, thousands of queer kids saw themselves reflected in the greater world for the first time, and that's something to be proud of.

By the way, I saw you once, at a book signing for your

autobiography. You didn't know it, of course, but it was an honor to finally meet you.

Anyhow, thank you for what you did, and what you have done over the last half-century. You changed many lives.

Best,

I.H. Tragitto

I stare at the letter for a long time.

It's unbelievable. The inherent paradoxes… I would have rejected stories that left so much hanging in the gap between times.

And yet, I'd *lived* it.

I close my eyes and try to remember him… how many signings did I do? How many old gay men came to them?

Then I remember the tall, spindly woman whom I'd assumed was trans who shook my hand at a reading in Paramus. She'd smiled shyly and said, "Thank you for publishing '*Firetime*.'" I'd thought it was a bit odd. She was the right age to have read it, but "Firetime" was about a couple gay protagonists. *The Seventh Gender* would have been more likely to spark her interest.

It was her. I know it now as surely as I know my own name.

All this time I'd assumed Tragitto was a man—the author had used a masculine name, after all—and my own biases hadn't let me consider another possibility.

I pull a bottle of Jamison out of my desk drawer and pour a finger of it into a clean glass. I lift it up and nod. "Here's to you, Ian."

I take a long sip, and it warms my gut.

I pull down the framed 'zine and set it carefully in the banker's box with the rest of my things. For just a moment, I can feel Jason standing there next to me, his arm around my waist.

Then he's gone. I check my tie in the mirror—the lightning hologram sizzles in the darkness—and grin.

"You ready?"

Daniel is leaning in the doorway, my husband of fifteen years, though we've been together for twenty-five. I still call him *NotMyFault* when we're alone.

Without Ian, we never would have met.

"Yup. Let's go. Can't keep them all waiting any longer." I picked up my box and kissed his cheek. I wave off the light and leave my office for the last time, off to celebrate my retirement.

What a story I have to tell you.

About Prolepsis

PROLEPSIS IS the last of the stories in this collection that was inspired by a word I ran across in my literary travels. Prolepsis means "the representation of a thing as existing before it actually does or did so."

Which got me thinking—what if I'd known what I know now about gender and sexual identity back in the eighties?

Which took me back to my high school years—high tops, flipped up collars, and boom boxes. I hope you had as much fun reading it as I did writing it."

ABOUT THE AUTHOR

I live with my husband of 28 years in a Sacramento, California suburb, in a little yellow house with a brick fireplace and a couple pink flamingoes.

As a writer, I've always lived between *here and now* and *what could be*. Indoctrinated into fantasy-sci fi by my mother at the tender age of nine, I devoured her library. But as I grew up and read the golden age classics and modern works, I began to wonder where the people like me were.

After I came out at twenty three, I decided it was time to create stories I couldn't find at Waldenbooks. If there weren't many gay characters in my favorite genres, I would reimagine them myself, populating them with men who loved men. I would subvert them and remake them to my own ends. And if I was lucky enough, someone else would want to read them.

My friends say my brain works a little differently—I see relationships between things that others miss, and get more done in a day than most folks manage in a week. Although I was born an introvert, I learned to reach outside himself and connect with others like me.

I write stories that subvert expectations, and transform sci fi, fantasy, and contemporary worlds into something new and unexpected. I run, Queer Sci Fi, QueeRomance Ink and Liminal Fiction with Mark, sites that bring people like us together to promote and celebrate fiction that reflects us.

I was recognized as one of the top new gay authors in the 2017 Rainbow Awards, and my debut novel "Skythane" received two awards. In 2019, I won Rainbow Awards for three other books, and became full member of the Science Fiction and Fantasy Writers of America in 2020.

My writing, whether queer romance or genre fiction (or a little bit of both) brings LGBTQ+ energy to my stories, infusing them with love, beauty and power and making them soar. I imagine a world that *could be*, and in the process, maybe changes the world that is just a little.

ALSO BY J. SCOTT COATSWORTH

Liminal Sky: Ariadne Cycle

The Stark Divide | The Rising Tide | The Shoreless Sea

Liminal Sky: Redemption Cycle

Dropnauts

Liminal Sky: Oberon Cycle

Skythane | Lander | Ithani

Other Sci Fi/Fantasy

The Autumn Lands | Cailleadhama | Firedrake | The Great North | Homecoming | The Last Run | Spells & Stardust Anthology | Wonderland

Contemporary/Magical Realism

Between the Lines | I Only Want to Be With You | Flames | The River City Chronicles | Slow Thaw

99¢ Shorts

Translation

Audiobooks

Cailleadhama | The Autumn Lands

LIKE WHAT YOU JUST READ?

Enjoy the first chapter of "The Stark Divide," Book One of the Liminal Sky: Ariadne Cycle.

Grab it now at Amazon

PROLOGUE

Lex floated along with the ocean current. Her arms were spread out wide, her jet-black hair adrift on the surface of the water. For once, she felt at peace. Truly herself.

The sun shone above her, and she soaked up its rays, basking in its golden glow. Her blue eyes stared up at the equally blue sky, not a cloud in sight. Soon she'd be called back to duty. Soon she'd once again have to face her limited, jury-rigged day-to-day existence. For a few moments, she was free to just drift.

The *Dressler*, a Mission-class AmSplor ship, sailed toward a city-sized rock named 43 Ariadne, harvested from the asteroid belt and placed in trailing orbit behind Earth. The starfish-shaped ship flew on the solar wind, drinking in ionized hydrogen and other trace elements that allowed her to breathe and grow, coursing slowly through the dark reaches of space between Earth and the sun. The *Dressler* lived on solar wind and space dust, accumulating them with her web of gossamer sails between her arms, filtering them down into her compact body for processing.

The detritus flew out behind her, leaving a jet trail across the void to mark her passing, leading back to Earth. Somewhere out there, their destination awaited them, an asteroid floating on a sea of stars.

CHAPTER 1 - THE THREE

"*DRESSLER*, SCHEMATIC," Colin McAvery, ship's captain and a third of the crew, called out to the ship-mind.

A three-dimensional image of the ship appeared above the smooth console. Her five living arms, reaching out from her central core, were lit with a golden glow, and the mechanical bits of instrumentation shone in red. In real life, she was almost two hundred meters from tip to tip.

Between those arms stretched her solar wings, a ghostly green film like the sails of the *Flying Dutchman*.

"You're a pretty thing," he said softly. He loved these ships, their delicate beauty as they floated through the starry void.

"Thank you, Captain." The ship-mind sounded happy with the compliment—his imagination running wild. Minds didn't have real emotions, though they sometimes approximated them.

He cross-checked the heading to be sure they remained on course to deliver their payload, the man-sized seed that was being dragged on a tether behind the ship. Humanity's ticket to the stars at a time when life on Earth was getting rapidly worse.

All of space was spread out before him, seen through the clear expanse of plasform set into the ship's living walls. His own face, trimmed blond hair, and deep brown eyes, stared back at him, superimposed over the vivid starscape.

At thirty, Colin was in the prime of his career. He was a starship captain, and yet sometimes he felt like little more than a bus driver. After this run… well, he'd have to see what other opportunities might be awaiting him. Maybe the doc was right, and this was the start of a whole new chapter for mankind. They might need a guy like him.

The walls of the bridge emitted a faint but healthy golden glow, providing light for his work at the curved mechanical console that filled half the room. He traced out the T-Line to their destination. "*Dressler*, we're looking a little wobbly." Colin frowned. Some irregularity in the course was common—the ship was constantly adjusting its trajectory—but she usually corrected it before he noticed.

"Affirmative, Captain." The ship-mind's miniature chosen likeness appeared above the touch board. She was all professional today, dressed in a standard AmSplor uniform, dark hair pulled back in a bun, and about a third life-sized.

The image was nothing more than a projection of the ship-mind, a fairy tale, but Colin appreciated the effort she took to humanize her appearance. Artificial mind or not, he always treated minds with respect.

"There's a blockage in arm four. I've sent out a scout to correct it."

The *Dressler* was well into slowdown now, her pre-arrival phase as she bled off her speed, and they expected to reach 43 Ariadne in another fifteen hours.

Pity no one had yet cracked the whole hyperspace thing. Colin chuckled. Asimov would be disappointed. "*Dressler*, show me Earth, please."

A small blue dot appeared in the middle of his screen.

"*Dressler*, three dimensions, a bit larger, please." The beautiful blue-green world spun before him in all its glory.

Appearances could be deceiving. Even with scrubbers working tirelessly night and day to clean the excess carbon dioxide from the air, the home world was still running dangerously warm.

He watched the image in front of him as the East Coast of the North American Union spun slowly into view. Florida was a sliver of its former self, and where New York City's lights had once shone, there was now only blue. If it *had* been night, Fargo, the capital of the Northern States, would have outshone most of the other cities below. The floods that had wiped out many of the world's coastal cities had also knocked down Earth's population, which was only now reaching the levels it had seen in the early twenty-first century.

All those new souls had been born into a warm, arid world.

We did it to ourselves. Colin, who had known nothing besides the hot planet he called home, wondered what it had been like those many years before *the Heat*.

Anastasia Anatov leafed through her father, Dimitri's, old paper journal. She liked to look through it once a day, to see his spidery handwriting and remember what he had been like. It was a bit old and dusty now, but it was one of her most cherished possessions.

She sighed and put it away in a storage nook in her lab.

She left the room and pulled herself gracefully along the runway, the central corridor of the ship, using the metal rungs embedded in the walls. She was much more comfortable in low or zero g than she was in Earth normal, where her tall, lanky form made her feel awkward around others. She was a loner at heart, and the emptiness of space appealed to her.

Her father had designed the Mission-class ships. It was something she rarely spoke of, but she was intensely proud of him. These ships were still imperfect, the combination of a hellishly complicated genetic code and after-the-fact fittings of mechanical parts, like the rungs she used now to move through the weightless environment.

Did it hurt when someone drilled into the living tissue to install mechanics, living quarters, and observation blisters? Her father had always maintained that the ship-minds felt no pain. She wasn't so sure. Men were often dismissive of the things they didn't understand.

Either way, she was stuck on the small ship for the duration with two men, neither of whom were interested in her. The captain was gay, and Jackson was married.

Too bad the ship roster hadn't included another woman or two.

She placed her hand on a hardened sensor callus next to the door valve and the ship obliged, recognizing her. The door spiraled open to show the viewport beyond.

She pulled herself into the room and floated before the wide expanse of transparent plasform, staring out at the seed being hauled behind them.

Nothing else mattered. Whatever she had to do to get this project launched, she would do it. She'd already made some morally questionable choices along the way—including looking the other way when a bundle of cash had changed hands at the Institute.

She was so close now, and she couldn't let anything get in the way.

Earth was a lost cause. It was only a matter of time before the world imploded. Only the seeds could give mankind a fighting chance to go on.

From the viewport, there was little to see. The seed was a two-meter-long brown ovoid, made of a hard, dark organic material, scarred and pitted by the continual abrasion of the dust that escaped the great sails. So cold out there, but the seed was dormant, unfeeling. The cold would keep it that way until the time came for its seedling stage.

She'd created three of the seeds with her funding. This one, bound for the asteroid 43 Ariadne, was the first. It was the next step in evolution beyond the *Dressler* and carried with it the hopes of all humankind.

It also represented ten years of her life and work.

Maybe, just maybe, we're ready for the next step.

THE CREW's third and final member, Jackson Hammond, hung upside down in the ship's hold, grunting as he refit one of the feed pipes that carried the ship's electronics through the bowels of this weird animal-mechanical hybrid. Although "up" and "down" were slight on a ship where the centrifugal force created a "gravity" only a fraction of what it was on Earth.

As the ship's engineer, Jackson was responsible for keeping the mechanics functioning—a challenge in a living organism like the *Dressler*.

With cold, hard metal, one dealt with the occasional metal fatigue, poor workmanship, and at times just ass-backward reality. But the parts didn't regularly grow or shrink, and it wasn't always necessary to rejigger the ones that had fit perfectly just the day before. Even after ten years in these things, he still found it a little creepy to be riding inside the belly of the beast. It was too Jonah and the Whale for his taste.

Jackson rubbed the sweat away from his eyes with the back of his arm. As he shaved down the end of a pipe to make it fit more snugly against the small orifice in the ship's wall, he touched the little silver cross that hung around his neck. It had been a present from his priest, Father Vincenzo, at his son Aaron's First Communion in the Reformed Catholic Evangelical Church.

The boy was seven years old now, with a shock of red hair and green eyes like his dad, and his mother's beautiful skin. He'd spent months preparing for his Communion Day, and Jackson remembered fondly the moment when his son had taken the Body and Blood of Christ for the first time, surprise registering on his little face at the strange taste of the wine.

Aaron's Communion Day had been a high point for Jackson, just a week before his current mission. He was so proud of his two boys. *Miss you guys. I'll be home soon.*

Lately he hadn't been sleeping well, his dreams filled with a dark-haired, blue-eyed vixen. He was happily married. He shouldn't be having such dreams.

Jackson shook his head. Being locked up in a tin can in space did strange things to a person sometimes. *I should be home with Glory and the boys.*

One way or another, this mission would be his last.

He'd been recruited as a teen.

At thirteen, Jackson had learned the basics of engineering doing black-tech work for the gangs that ran what was left of the Big Apple after the Rise—a warren of interconnected skyrises, linked mostly by boats and ropes and makeshift bridges.

Everything north of Twenty-Third was controlled by the Hex, a black-tech co-op that specialized in bootlegged dreamcasts, including modified versions that catered to some of the more questionable tastes of the North American States. South of Twenty-

Third belonged to the Red Badge, a lawless group of technophiles involved in domestic espionage and wetware arts.

Jackson had grown up in the drowned city, abandoned by his mother and forced to rely on his own intelligence and instincts to survive in a rapidly changing world.

He'd found his way to the Red Badge and discovered a talent for ecosystem work, taking over and soon expanding one of the rooftop farms that supplied the drowned city with a subsistence diet. An illegal wetware upgrade let him tap directly into the systems he worked on, seeing the circuits and pathways in his head.

He increased the Badge's food production fivefold and branched out beyond the nearly tasteless molds and edible fungi that thrived in the warm, humid environment.

It was on one of his rooftop "gardens" that his life had changed one warm summer evening.

He was underneath one of the condenser units that pulled water from the air for irrigation. All of eighteen years old, he was responsible for the food production for the entire Red Badge.

He'd run through the unit's diagnostics app to no avail. Damned piece of shit couldn't find a thing wrong.

In the end, it had come down to something purely physical—tightening down a pipe bolt where the condenser interfaced with the irrigation system.

Satisfied with the work, he stood, wiping the sweat off his bare chest, and glared into the setting sun out over the East River. It was more an inland sea now, but the old names still stuck.

There was a faint whirring behind him, and he spun around. A bug drone hovered about a foot away, glistening in the sun. He stared at it for a moment, then reached out to swat it down. Probably from the Hex.

It evaded his grasp, and he felt a sharp pain in his neck.

He went limp, and everything turned black as he tumbled into one of his garden beds.

He awoke in Fargo, recruited by AmSplor to serve in the space agency's Frontier Station, his life changed irrevocably.

A strange sensation brought him back to the present.

His right hand was wet. Startled, he looked down. It was covered with blood.

Dressler, *we have a problem*, he said through his private affinity-link with the ship-mind.

Grab it now at Amazon

CPSIA information can be obtained
at www.ICGtesting.com
Printed in the USA
BVHW060733200122
626629BV00013B/1473